"Y... Sal exclaimed.

"Yes," Annie responded. "I should start getting on with my life. And it's about time you stopped feeling so obligated to me. You've been wonderf—"

"I don't feel obligated," he said firmly, clenching his jaw. Obligation had nothing to do with what he was feeling at the moment; it was out-and-out jealousy. "Besides, you don't know anything about this guy."

"And how much do you know about the women you go out with?" Annie shot back, beginning to lose her temper. "Generally not much more than the fact that their measurements are bigger than their IQ's."

"That's different."

"Why is it different?" she cried, taking a threatening step closer to him. "And if you tell me it's because you're a man, Sal, I'll—I'll...bop you!"

"Annie," Sal said with a grin, "are you threatening a police officer?"

"Yes!"

As their eyes met and held, Annie swallowed, feeling flustered. Something was happening here that she didn't quite understand. This was Smooth, Suave Sal, Annie cautioned herself. *You'd better watch yourself.*

Dear Reader:

Happy holidays! All the best wishes to you for a joyful, loving holiday season with your family and friends.

And while celebrating, I hope that you think of Silhouette Romance. Our authors join me in wishing you a wonderful holiday season, and we have some treats in store for you during November and December—as well as during the exciting new year.

Experience the magic that makes the world so special for two people falling in love. Meet heroines who will make you cheer for their happiness and heroes (be they the boy next door or a handsome, mysterious stranger) who will win your heart. Silhouette Romances reflect the magic of love—sweeping you away with books that will make you laugh and cry, heartwarming, poignant stories that will move you time and time again.

During the next months, we're publishing romances by many of your all-time favorites such as Diana Palmer, Brittany Young, Lucy Gordon and Victoria Glenn. Your response to these authors and others in Silhouette Romances has served as a touchstone for us, and we're pleased to bring you more books with Silhouette's distinctive medley of charm, wit and—above all—*romance*.

I hope you enjoy this book and the many stories to come. Come home to Silhouette romance—for always!

Sincerely,

Tara Hughes
Senior Editor
Silhouette Books

SHARON DE VITA

Italian
Knights

Silhouette *Romance*
Published by Silhouette Books New York
America's Publisher of Contemporary Romance

This book is dedicated to three generations of
Italian Knights:

My father-in-law, Reverend Frank De Vita, with special
thanks for all his "technical assistance" and his memories
of Italy.

My husband, Tony, with special thanks for being the
inspiration not only for this book, but for them all.

My son, Anthony, with special thanks for teaching me to
believe in miracles.

SILHOUETTE BOOKS
300 E. 42nd St., New York, N.Y. 10017

ISBN: 0-373-08610-5

First Silhouette Books printing November 1988

All the characters in this book are fictitious. Any
resemblance to actual persons, living or dead, is
purely coincidental.

®: Trademark used under license and
registered in the United States Patent and
Trademark Office and in other countries.

Printed in the U.S.A.

Books by Sharon De Vita

Silhouette Romance

Heavenly Match #475
Lady and the Legend #498
Kane and Mabel #545
Baby Makes Three #573
Sherlock's Home #593
Italian Knights #610

SHARON DE VITA

decided around her thirtieth birthday that she wanted to produce something that didn't have to be walked or fed during the night. An eternal optimist who always believes in happy endings, she felt romances were the perfect vehicle for her creative energies. As a reader, and a writer, she prefers stories that are fun and light-hearted, and tries to inject these qualities in her own work. The mother of three, she has been happily married to her high school sweetheart for eighteen years.

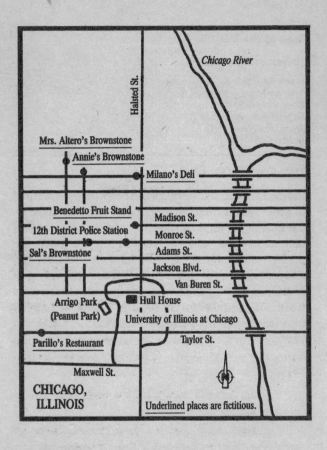

Chicago River

Halsted St.

Mrs. Altero's Brownstone

Annie's Brownstone

Milano's Deli

Benedetto Fruit Stand

Madison St.

12th District Police Station

Monroe St.

Sal's Brownstone

Adams St.

Jackson Blvd.

Van Buren St.

Arrigo Park
(Peanut Park)

Hull House

University of Illinois at Chicago

Parillo's Restaurant

Taylor St.

Maxwell St.

CHICAGO,
ILLINOIS

Underlined places are fictitious.

Chapter One

"Sal?" Annie called, bumping the front door open with her hip as she juggled two bags of groceries. "Is that you?"

"Shh," he hissed, reaching one long arm out to slam the door shut behind her.

"Sal!" Annie cried as he yanked the bags out of her arms and pulled her down on the floor beside him. "What *are* you doing?"

"Hiding," he whispered, leaning up to peek out the window again.

"I can see that," Annie complained. Craning her neck, she tried to follow his line of vision, but Sal pushed her back down and hunkered his six-foot frame closer to the floor. It was hard to squish a six-foot frame under a window ledge that was three feet high, but he was trying.

"Who are we hiding from?" Annie whispered, wondering what kind of mischief he'd gotten himself into now.

"Oh, no!" Sal groaned. "Here she comes."

"Here *who* comes?" Exasperated, Annie struggled to sit up, but Sal held her down.

"Mrs. Altero," he whispered. He was checking out the street as if he were on surveillance. "Her granddaughter's visiting from Italy, and Mrs. Altero wants me to come to dinner to meet her." Sal groaned softly. "I love Mrs. Altero dearly, but Annie, I don't think I can take any more of her cooking."

Annie laughed softly. Mrs. Altero was the neighborhood matchmaker. She was a wonderful woman with a kind heart and a loving spirit, but she was also the world's worst cook. No one in the neighborhood had the heart to tell her, so they just endured her gastronomic oddities in silence.

"Poor Sal." Shaking her head, Annie clucked her tongue sympathetically. "It's your own fault," she teased. "Haven't I been telling you, if you're not careful one of those ladies who's always chasing you is going to catch you?"

"Not me," Sal quipped, his dark eyes twinkling with mischief. "The only woman *I*'m ever going to have a serious relationship with is Sara Lee. I'm as slippery as greased lightning, and just as quick." He eased himself up and peeked through the window again. "Thank God. She's gone." Heaving a sigh of relief, Sal relaxed against the wall and wiped an imaginary bead of sweat off his forehead.

Annie couldn't help it, she grinned.

"What's so funny?" he asked, the barest hint of a smile curling his lips.

"Nothing," she lied, her smile going wider. Poor Sal. Ruggedly handsome with a head of thick curly black hair and piercing dark eyes, he had a lazy, knock-em-dead smile and an easygoing personality that had women everywhere throwing themselves at his feet. His rough-hewn elegance only added to his allure. No wonder little old ladies tried to feed him dinner—and their granddaughters.

"Can I get up now?" she asked, leaning on his shoulder for balance. "I'd love to play hide-and-seek with you, Detective Giordiano, but I'm in a hurry."

"In a hurry?" Scooping up her groceries Sal rolled to his feet. "My God, Annie!" He leaned down to peer into her startled face. "What on earth did you do to your hair?"

"I got it cut," she said dryly, wondering what the devil Sal was frowning about.

"What did you do that for?" He'd known Annie for years, but he had never really noticed how beautiful she was until this very moment. Her hair had been her crowning glory, a curtain of black velvet that cascaded down her back, nearly reaching her waist. Now it framed her delicate face in a curly halo, making her eyes look larger and more luminous than ever.

"Don't you like it?" she asked hesitantly, arching her neck to meet his gaze. Sal's frown deepened.

"Well…I guess so. It's…I…I'm just not used to it. And what's your hurry?" he asked, arching one dark brow suspiciously.

Annie grinned. "I've got a date."

"A date!" Sal's brows drew together. "What do you mean you have a date? What *kind* of date?"

"The usual kind," she assured him, trying to banish a smile at the stunned look on his face. "With a man." She tried to retrieve her groceries, but he wouldn't let go. Annie sighed in exasperation.

"Sal?" Deliberately she softened her voice. "It's been nearly two years since Tony died. Don't you think it's time for me to get on with the business of living?"

It had been two long years since her husband's death and Annie knew it was time to stop living in the past, and get on with her future. She knew it, but she wasn't quite sure Sal did. As her husband's best friend and former partner, Sal had become her tower of strength, a friendly shoulder to cry on. As tempting as it was to always lean on him, Annie knew she couldn't do it forever. Sal had to get on with his own life, too, and she knew Sal wouldn't do that unless he was certain she could handle things on her own. Dating again was her own way of showing him she could take care of herself. Despite Sal's reputation as a womanizer, he was one of the kindest, sweetest men she had ever known. But she was tired of being his personal burden, no matter how good a friend he had been to her husband. Or to her.

"You're going out with a *man*?" Sal repeated incredulously, as if she'd just announced she was planning a one-woman assault on some top-secret military installation.

Annie rolled her eyes to the heavens. "Yes, with a man!" Her back went up. "Believe it or not, Sal, I'm twenty-six years old. I'm not *quite* over-the-hill yet. A man is actually interested in taking me out. Now I know that might come as a shock to you, but—"

"That's not what I mean, Annie." Sal shook his dark head slowly, as if trying to assimilate all this information. "I...it's not a shock, it's just... well...Annie, you never said anything to *me* about this." His tone of voice clearly indicated he thought this an obvious breach of social etiquette.

"Now Sal," Annie admonished gently, noting the grave look on his handsome features. "Do you tell me every time you have a date?"

"That's...different," Sal retorted vaguely, and Annie's dark brows rose a fraction.

"Different?" she repeated, cocking her head to look at him. "And why, may I ask, is that different?"

"Because."

"Because why?" she persisted, and Sal shifted his large frame uncomfortably.

"Just...*because*," he insisted with an airy wave of his hand. Her dark eyes narrowed and she looked at him carefully.

"Let me get this straight," Annie said slowly, feeling her temper rise. "It's all right for *you* to go out carousing every night, but not me. Is that right?"

"Right," he confirmed. His jaw tightened. "And what do you mean *carousing*!" he thundered. "You said this was a date, *you never said anything about carousing*!"

Annie ground her teeth together. She'd been in mourning longer than she'd been married, long enough for the pain to fade to a distant memory, so why was Sal acting as if it were a sacrilege that she was going out on a date? "Would you mind telling me why it's all right for *you* to go out, but not for me?"

"Because I'm a man," he returned, as if that explained everything.

"Because you're a—" Annie inhaled deeply. "Just what the hell is that supposed to mean?" she cried, furious at his sexist remark.

"Don't swear, Ann Marie," Sal instructed, using her given name to show his annoyance.

"Salvatore Giordiano," she snapped, glaring up into his face. "I'm twenty-six years old. I've buried my mother, my father *and* my husband. I think I've earned the right to swear if I want to!"

Sal heaved a deep, exasperated sigh that stretched his shirt taut across rippling muscles. His suit jacket was slung carelessly over his shoulder, and his tie hung at half-mast, circling the massive column of his neck. He looked tired and perplexed, and about as confused as she'd ever seen him.

"Sal," she began carefully. "Do you have some objection to me dating?"

He looked at her and felt his gut tighten. Annie and another guy! Damn! He knew eventually she would start dating again. It was only natural. She was a young, beautiful woman and had a lot to offer. It was just that he hadn't expected it—at least not so soon. In his mind he *knew* the day would come eventually, but the idea of Annie with some guy—any guy—made him feel like hitting something.

"No," he lied, absently scratching the back of his neck. "I guess I don't have any objections. I'm just . . . surprised." Sal tried to force a smile he didn't feel. "How did you meet this . . . *guy*?" he inquired, deliberately making her date sound like some errant strand of virus she'd unintentionally picked up somewhere.

"He was interested in buying the store—"

"Buying the store!" Sal bellowed. "You didn't tell me you were selling the store," he accused, his deep, gravelly voice tinged with intense annoyance. Annie shook her head and rolled her eyes toward the heavens. The Milano deli had been in her family for three generations; it was practically a landmark in the old Italian neighborhood known as Little Italy where they lived. The deli sat on a prime piece of real estate, and despite the numerous—and generous—offers she'd received, Sal knew she would never sell it.

"I'm not selling the store," she explained patiently. "I never *had* any intention of selling the store. But David didn't know that until he came in to inquire. After I told him I wasn't interested in selling, we started talking and—" she shrugged, wondering why she suddenly felt so defensive "—he asked me for a date."

Sal's face darkened and a muscle along his cheek jerked. "Do you mean to tell me," he thundered, "that you're going out with some . . . some . . . *stranger* who just happened to mosey on into the store?" Anger thickened his voice, giving it a deep, gritty texture Annie felt all the way down to her toes.

"He's not a stranger," she protested, wondering why on earth Sal was treating her like a rebellious twelve-year-old.

"Just what do you know about this...*Duntley* guy?"

Annie's eyes slid closed. "His name is David," she corrected, knowing Sal was deliberately trying to be obtuse to aggravate her. "And he's in real estate," she added, as if that were a wealth of information. Annie could see he was struggling for control. He jammed a hand through his dark hair and started again.

"Do you mean to tell me," he said carefully, "that you are going out on a date with a man you know nothing about!"

"Oh, for goodness' sake," Annie cried in exasperation. "Are you feeling all right?" She reached out to touch his forehead for signs of a fever. Sal drew back and gave her a stern look.

"This isn't funny, Annie. You don't even know this man—"

"Sal," she cried, trying not to laugh at the intensity in his face. "I'm going on a date, Sal. Nothing more, nothing less. It's not a lifelong commitment. We're going to have dinner, go dancing, maybe even go park for a while," she teased, her dark eyes alight with mischief in an effort to make him see the ridiculousness of the situation.

"Park!" Sal thundered, obviously seeing nothing of the kind. "I'm going to check this guy out," he barked, pushing past her.

"Oh, no, you're not! You are *not* going to play detective with my date," Annie cried, grabbing his arm. She knew how intimidating Sal could be when he put his mind to it. "I'm perfectly capable of handling my own life and my own *affairs*."

Affairs. The word reverberated around the silent room, bouncing off the walls and echoing over and over. Oh, Lord. Annie swallowed hard. "Sal... It's—that's not—that's not what I meant," she stammered weakly as he drew himself up to his full height, expelling a deep, exasperating breath.

"Ann Marie," he said gravely. "Just what has gotten into you?"

"Into me?" she cried, resisting the urge to whack him. "You're the one whose behavior is so peculiar! What on earth is wrong with you?" She glared up at him, and he glared right back. For long, silent moments they stared at each other.

A sudden thought occurred to Annie and she immediately felt contrite. Oh, Lord, why hadn't she realized it sooner?

Of course Sal would be upset that she was dating again. Perhaps in his mind, he felt as if she were being disloyal to Tony's memory. Sal and Tony had grown up together, they'd been closer than brothers, naturally Sal would be upset about her reentry into society.

"Sal," she said softly, reaching out to touch his arm. "I'm sorry, I didn't realize—" Annie lowered her gaze. Why hadn't she been more sensitive? She should have known that Sal would feel uncomfortable about her dating again. Perhaps she shouldn't have just dropped it on him; she should have eased into it a bit more slowly. She had to let Sal know that her dating, her getting back into life was in no way an act of disloyalty. What it was, was her own declaration of independence, an act that would set Sal free. She'd leaned on him long enough.

Despite Sal's reputation as a womanizer, he had an old-fashioned sense of honor and loyalty, and that was one of the things she'd always respected about him. But she wouldn't use his sense of honor to tie him to her anymore. Two years was long enough for him to carry the burden of her widowhood.

Annie had loved her husband, and it had hurt when he died. But there was a time for grieving, and a time for living. The pain of Tony's death had eased to a distant memory; they'd been married for almost a year and a half; she'd been in mourning for longer than that. And to no one, not even Sal, would she admit that her marriage hadn't been perfect. What good would it do now? It was in the past. All she could do was go forward. If only she could make Sal understand.

"Sal," she began gently. "I know how you felt about Tony. But it's been two years. He's gone and there's nothing anyone can do to change that. It's time for me to get on with my life. Just because I'm dating, please don't think I'm being disloyal to him. You know it's what he would have wanted. Tony wouldn't have wanted me to be alone the rest of my life."

"But, honey, you're not alone," Sal protested. "I'm here."

"Sal," she said, suddenly understanding his concern. "I can't lean on you the rest of my life."

"And why not?" he demanded, inclining his head to look at her. "If I'm not complaining, I don't see why you're—"

"Sal—" Annie took a deep breath. "—it's time for me to stand on my own two feet. Don't think I don't appreciate all you've done for me. I do. I don't know how I would have gotten through those first awful months without you." Smiling, she touched his arm. "But you've got your own life to lead. I certainly can't expect you to sit around here holding my hand for the rest of my life."

"But, it's just so sudden," Sal said, clearly unimpressed with her reasoning. The honeyed gentleness of his voice caused a ripple of warmth to shimmy over her. His eyes held hers and her pulse quickened in response.

"Sal, please try to understand. I don't want you to feel obligated to me. You've been wonder—"

"I don't feel obligated," he said firmly, clenching his jaw. Obligation had nothing to do with what he was feeling at the moment. He hated to admit that what he was feeling right now was nothing but out-and-out jealousy.

"Sal, look," Annie said tiredly, running a hand through her newly permed locks. "I'm sorry, I shouldn't have dropped this on you so suddenly. But it just happened. I met David, and it wasn't like I planned it—"

"But you don't know anything about this guy," Sal protested, and Annie heaved a weary sigh. He was back to that again.

"What if he's a mugger?" Sal challenged, working up a head of steam just at the thought. "This guy could have a police record, for all you know. I can't believe you'd actually agree to go out with a man you don't know anything about!'' He shook his head as if she'd suddenly taken leave of her senses.

"Sal Giordiano," Annie cried, losing what was left of her temper. "If that isn't the pot calling the kettle black! How much do you know about the women you go out with? Generally not much more than the fact that their measurements are bigger than their IQ.'' Standing toe-to-toe, they glared at each other, neither willing to back down.

"That's different," Sal barked, and Annie clenched her fists together.

"And why is it different?'' she cried, taking a threatening step closer to him. "And if you tell me it's because you're a man, Sal, I'll—I'll—'' she searched for some appropriate action ''—I'll bop you,'' she threatened, shaking her fist at him.

"Annie!" Sal said with a grin, grabbing her fist and holding on tight. "Are you threatening a police officer?''

"Yes!'' she confirmed, scowling at the sudden warmth that engulfed her from his touch.

Sal cocked his head to look at her intently. He'd never met a woman like her. She was one of a kind, beautiful and gentle, yet she could hold her own with any man.

His eyes suddenly fastened on the moistness of her mouth. His muscles tensed in response. A sudden, fierce urge to tug her close and cover her lips with his caused an unexpected stirring in his loins. What the hell was the matter with him? This was Tony's widow, for God's sake!

Annie stared at him in confusion, watching a series of emotions play across Sal's face. There was a fierce gleam in his dark eyes, a gleam she didn't recognize and had never seen before. Bedroom eyes, Annie thought immediately, suddenly warmed by the image.

Flustered at her response, Annie pulled her hand free and took a self-conscious step back. Sal was looking at her—no, studying her—the way a man looks at a woman...an attractive woman. Oh, Lord, Annie thought suddenly. She'd seen Sal look at other women that way, but never at her. Annie swallowed hard, feeling unaccountably flustered.

Their eyes met and held, their faces suddenly only inches apart. Tension froze the air and Annie couldn't seem to breathe. She didn't dare. Something she didn't quite understand was happening here. It had been a long time since she'd had a man's...attention, but not so long that she didn't recognize it or respond to it.

Annie blinked, her thoughts frozen. Sal was close enough for her to feel his breath ruffle her hair. Why hadn't she ever noticed the rugged maleness of his after-shave, the rippling width of his shoulders, the way one dark curl dipped rakishly across his forehead?

Watch yourself, Annie, she cautioned herself, trying to ignore the increased tempo of her pulse. Sal was a friend—her best friend—and she shouldn't be having these romantic feelings about him.

"I...I have to put my groceries away," she stammered, trying to sidestep around him. She felt like running—anything—just to get away from the errant thoughts and feelings storming through her.

Sal dropped his hand and caught her arm the same way he'd done thousands of times. The gesture was achingly familiar, yet different somehow. The warmth of his skin enveloped hers and Annie self-consciously withdrew. Wide-eyed, she slowly raised her gaze to his, and her breath withered.

What on earth was the matter with her? She was suddenly responding to him like an adolescent in the throes of her first crush. This was good ole Sal.

But the look in his eyes wasn't quite what she'd expected from good ole Sal. Somehow, when she wasn't looking, good ole Sal had turned on the industrial-strength charm, and apparently she wasn't any more immune to it than any other woman.

"Annie."

Her lashes lowered at the gentleness of his voice. His touch sizzled her tender skin, causing her heart to thud recklessly in her breast.

The doorbell rang, shattering the quiet, and Annie jumped back guiltily. She shook her head, trying to loosen the cobwebs and put things in perspective. It was only natural for her to be nervous, she decided, blaming her sudden attack of anxiety on the fact that she was going on a date. She hadn't been on a date in years. What she was feeling had nothing to do with Sal, she insisted to herself. Nothing at all.

Annie dropped her poor, ragged grocery bags onto a table and turned toward the door. Lord, it was probably David and she hadn't even changed yet. She still had on her white deli apron over a pair of faded jeans and a shirt. At least her hair was fixed, she thought dully, absently touching her new curls.

"Annie, wait."

A shiver rippled over her as Sal dropped his hand to her shoulder, jolting her poor nerve endings into spasms of shock. She didn't dare turn; she didn't trust herself. Sal was too close, and she too flustered. Without a word, Sal reached around her but Annie planted her foot in front of the door to prevent him from opening it.

"What do you think you're doing?" she said angrily, trying unsuccessfully to push past him and keep her foot on the door at the same time.

"I'm just going to answer the door," Sal told her sweetly, his eyes glinting in amusement. "I want to meet this...stranger before you go waltzing off into the night with him. You don't mind, do you?" he asked, his tone of voice indicating it was just too bad if she did.

"I'm warning you," Annie whispered, ducking under his arm and turning to glare up into his face. "You'd better behave yourself, and none of that macho police bull, either. David is a very nice man, and I don't want you scaring him."

"Now, Annie, would I do that?" Sal inquired, managing to look quite innocent. She heaved a weary sigh.

"Sal, please?"

Grinning, Sal bent down and pulled the curtain back.

"Now what are you doing?" Annie cried, mortified that he was spying on her date.

"Oh, my God!" Sal groaned, craning his neck for a better look at David. "Annie, what the hell kind of a guy are you going out with?" He turned to look at her, his face aghast. "This guy has a skirt on!"

Chapter Two

What! Let me see," Annie demanded, elbowing Sal out of the way to do a little spying of her own. Her eyes widened in disbelief. "Cow cakes!" she muttered. David had on what she recognized as a traditional ethnic costume. At least she *hoped* it was a costume. He wore a tartan kilt, a white shirt, knee socks and shiny little round-toed shoes. The entire ensemble was capped off by a jaunty little plaid tam that was perched directly on top of his slightly balding head.

Good Lord, Annie thought, staring at him in disbelief. His outfit was prettier than hers. Her mother had always told her never to date a man she could swap clothes with. At the moment, Annie wished she could take her mother's advice.

"It's not a skirt, Sal. It's a kilt," she clarified, although she didn't know why she bothered. Skirt. Kilt.

From the expression on Sal's face, she could tell he wasn't in the least bit interested in the specifics of David's attire. Sal looked as if he'd managed to identify it all on his own.

Why on earth did David choose this particular evening to wear that blasted thing? Annie wondered darkly. If Sal was concerned about her going out with David before, now he was practically frothing at the mouth.

"He's probably part of some radical fringe group," Sal muttered dubiously. His head was only inches from hers and Annie caught a faint whiff of his aftershave. Pleasant, intoxicating and definitely masculine. It suited Sal.

"He's got blue eyes," Sal informed her gravely, as if blue eyes were an arrestable offense. "And he sweats. You know I've never trusted a guy who sweats," he muttered, and Annie moaned softly.

"Sal, please? You're not making this any easier for me," she complained, trying to push past him. Sal bit back a smile. That was the whole idea.

Annie scowled as she peeked at poor, unsuspecting David again. For two cents she would send him back to wherever it was he came from. She no longer felt like going out with him, or anyone else, for that matter. It just wasn't worth the wear and tear on her nerves. But to back down now would only make Sal think he'd won. On principle alone she was going to go through with this date, just to prove to Sal that she could stand on her own two feet. It was for his own good, she assured herself. But somehow she had a feeling that Sal didn't see it that way.

"I don't know about this guy," Sal growled, shaking his head. "I don't like this, Annie. Not at all." He glanced at David again and felt an unfamiliar tightening in his belly. If Annie thought he was going to let her just up and waltz out of here with some guy she didn't know, who had a fondness for shiny little shoes and dancing skirts, she was in for a very rude surprise. Where on earth did she find this character? he wondered in disgust.

"Will you stop this?" Annie hissed. She could understand Sal's concern, but now he was carrying this protective bit too far. He was beginning to annoy her. "No wonder the poor man's sweating. He's probably nervous. Wouldn't you be if some menacing-looking man wearing a gun was peeking at you through a window? Now, I'm warning—"

"You're not leaving this house, Ann Marie," Sal said firmly, crossing his arms across his chest defiantly. He knew immediately that it was the wrong thing to say. He'd learned long ago to never, ever tell Annie she couldn't do something. You could ask, plead or cajole, but never *tell* her. Telling or ordering Annie to do something was like waving a red flag in front of a bull's face.

Her shoulders straightened and she drew herself to her full five-foot frame. "Salvatore," she said slowly, deciding this situation warranted the full use of his name. "Like it or not, I've made a date, and I'm going out with David tonight. If you want to stay and meet him, fine. You can entertain him while I change. But I'm warning you, Sal," she said, shaking one slender finger in his face, "you'd better behave."

"Me, behave?" Sal drew back and made a great show of checking his gun. His eyes filled with mischief. "I promise to be on my... best behavior."

She looked at him carefully, fearful of what was going through his cop's mind. Poor David, she thought a bit belatedly, wondering how he was going to react to Sal's intimidating presence. "Sal, I'm warning—"

"Come on, Annie," he encouraged, trying to fight her for the door. "You don't want to leave your...*date* just standing there, do you? It wouldn't be polite."

Leaving David outside might not be polite, but faced with the prospect of letting him in so Sal could breathe down his neck hardly seemed a pleasant alternative, either. Fluffing her hair, Annie gave Sal one last warning glance before taking a deep breath and pulling open the front door.

"David," she said with false cheer, elbowing Sal aside. "How nice to see you again. Please come in. I'm not quite ready yet." She babbled nervously, glancing at Sal quickly. "But I'm sure you won't mind waiting while I change. It will only take a moment."

David's face broke into a wide smile when he saw her. But the smile slowly slid off David's face when he caught sight of Sal, who stood firmly rooted in the doorway. His long legs were planted wide apart in a threatening stance that no doubt intimidated murderers and muggers alike.

"David," she said quickly, noting the way the two men were visually appraising one another. "I'd like you to meet Sal Giordiano. He's an old family friend. Sal, this is David Donaldson."

"It's nice to meet you," Sal said with a pathetic lack of sincerity. Annie rolled her eyes.

"Come on in," Sal invited, grabbing David's hand. Pumping hard, Sal gave David's hand a hearty yank, pulling him through the doorway and nearly off his pretty patent-leather feet.

Recovering his balance and composure, David turned to stare at Sal in dismay. David was a good five inches shorter than Sal, Annie noted, and as light and fair as Sal was dark. David had a rather round, nondescript face, and even more nondescript features, in direct contrast to Sal's. Sal's face was dark and intense; his jaw was firm, his eyes intelligent. Once someone saw Sal Giordiano, they never forgot him. His handsome features were forever etched in their memory.

David on the other hand was a face in a crowd. He was kind and nonthreatening, which is why she'd decided he would be a perfect man for her first date. To begin with, she was nervous enough about this whole business of dating.

The whole purpose of starting this dating fiasco was strictly so that Sal would realize she could stand on her own two feet, *and* so he wouldn't feel obligated to her anymore. Sal had his own life to live; and it was time he got on with the business of living it, without worrying about her.

If the truth be known, Annie wasn't sure she wanted to start playing the dating game again. She hadn't liked it the first time, when she was barely sixteen. At twenty-six, the prospect was even less thrilling.

But she was tired of being a weight around Sal's neck. If he thought she was dating someone, then maybe he would stop worrying about her. She hoped.

She'd planned to spend a nice quiet evening in the company of a nice, safe man. A man with whom she wouldn't have to worry about being pressured into any kind of romantic involvement. Annie knew she wasn't ready for that part, yet. Even though she'd only known David a few weeks, he seemed pleasant enough, if a bit pompous. Conversation with David would be light and meaningless, nothing intense or probing. Just what she needed right now. Annie had thought David would be perfect for her first date.

But now, watching Sal eye him like a fox after a hound, she wasn't quite so sure.

"I'm sorry about my outfit, Ann," David said with a smile, deliberately ignoring Sal. "But I play in a bugle corps, and we had a reception at a consulate this afternoon. I didn't have time to change, so I thought we could stop by my apartment on the way to dinner."

"One date and he's already taking you to his apartment!" Sal whispered in her ear. His warm breath teased her delicate skin and her senses warmed in immediate response. Annie flashed Sal a warning look. There was a long, awkward silence for a moment, as the men continued to appraise each other.

"So...David," Sal finally said, rocking back and forth on his heels and crossing his arms across his chest. "What do you do?"

"Do?" David stiffened, recognizing an interrogation when he saw one.

"For a living," Sal clarified.

"I'm in real estate. And you?" he inquired politely.

"Detective," Sal said succinctly, deliberately adjusting his shoulder holster while David eyed the gun.

"Do you...uh...carry your gun all the time?" the smaller man asked nervously.

Sal grinned. "Do you wear a skirt all the time?"

"Salvatore!" Annie exclaimed softly, wondering what the charges were for gagging a police officer. Whatever they were, she was ready to risk it.

"No." David shook his head, flashing Sal a patronizing smile. "Only on special occasions." He matched Sal stare for stare, apparently not in the least bit intimidated by him.

"I *always* carry my gun. You just never know when you might need a weapon." Sal's tone of voice indicated he expected to need his gun at any moment.

Oh, Lord. Annie shook her head, resisting the temptation to whack Sal. Again.

"David," Annie said abruptly, jumping in and trying to ease the tension between the two men. She didn't particularly care for this macho baloney. "Please make yourself at home. I have to change, but I'll only be a minute." She had second thoughts about leaving Sal and David alone, but she had no choice. She wasn't about to go out on her very first date in a smelly apron and jeans just because she was worried that two seemingly adult men couldn't behave themselves.

"Sal, could I see you for a moment?" she inquired with forced sweetness. She headed toward the stairs and Sal followed, occasionally glancing back at David.

"I'll be right back," Sal called over his shoulder, his words more a threat than a promise.

At the top of the steps, Annie whirled on him. "Sal," she began, working hard to hold on to her temper. "What on earth has come over you! You're acting like an overprotective father! I want you to stop it, right now! My *own father* didn't give me this much trouble when I went on my first date at sixteen."

"Well, maybe he should have," Sal said to annoy her. "What on earth do you see in this guy? He hardly seems your type."

"My type!" Annie cried. She immediately remembered David was downstairs and lowered her voice. "What is that supposed to mean? I don't have a...*type*! I didn't have one at sixteen and I don't have one now."

"See what I mean," Sal said smugly, flashing her a wicked grin that caused her heart to pound. "If you don't have a type, Annie, then how do you know you want to go out with this guy?"

She hated it when he insisted upon being reasonable. "I...I just know," Annie stammered, unable to think of one really good reason why she wanted to go out with David. She didn't have one. It wasn't as if he were her "type," but rather that he just happened to have asked her out. But she couldn't very well admit that to Sal. "David's very...nice, and...clean and..." Sal was standing so close, looking so mischievous, Annie forgot what she was saying.

"Nice and clean, huh?" One dark brow rose in amusement. "Well, Annie, I assure you, those are definitely sterling qualities, but hardly what I call a reason to go on a date with someone. Mrs. Altero's parrot is nice and clean, but I sure as hell wouldn't want to see you go on a date with him, either. Although, I must admit, the parrot does seem to have a bit more personality."

"Sal—" Annie rubbed a spot between her brow that had begun to throb "—I don't see what the big deal is," she whispered, leaning close so he could hear her. "What's all the fuss about one little date? If I didn't know better, I'd swear you were jealous!"

"Jealous!" Sal thundered, realizing how close to the truth she'd come. "Why the hell would I be jealous of that—that—"

Annie clamped her hand over his mouth. "Will you be quiet," she cried. "He'll hear you."

"Annie," Sal mumbled, pulling her hand free so he could speak. "What's your rush?" His eyes held hers. When he laced his fingers firmly through hers, Annie shivered as the warmth of his hand engulfed her, causing her pulse to quicken in response. Startled, she withdrew her hand. "There's no reason for you to run off with the first guy who asks you out." Sal was stalling for time, hoping against hope he could find a way to change her mind about going out with this guy. She'd hit too close to the truth about his being jealous.

"I'm not running off, and David is not the first guy to ask me out," Annie said, trying to banish a grin at the sudden alarmed look on his face.

"He's not?"

"For your information, Detective Giordiano," Annie began smugly, crossing her arms across her chest, "last week Mr. Finucci invited me to go the movies." Mr. Finucci was eighty-one years old, had one gold tooth and walked with the aid of a goat-handled cane. Mr. Finucci was also a champion boccie ball player. Despite his age, he still had an eye—his good one—for the ladies. He was not above sneaking a pinch when he felt the need. But, Annie mused, widows couldn't be choosers. A date was a date. And she loved Mr. Finucci dearly.

"Ahh," Sal drawled, his grin widening. "I always knew Mr. Finucci had good taste." He leaned forward and spoke directly into her face, unnerving her with his closeness. "At least I know Mr. Finucci. I don't know anything about this David character."

"He's not a character," she defended, growing irritated again. She wasn't certain if she was annoyed at Sal for his behavior, or with herself because of the strange reaction she was having to him.

"I have an idea," Sal said, suddenly brightening. "Why don't you just let me interrogate David a little? Just enough to put the fear of God into him? I'd feel much— Annie, why are you looking at me that way?"

Closing her eyes, Annie took a deep breath and struggled for control. "Sal, listen to me very carefully. You are *not* going to interrogate David, nor are you going to put the fear of God into him or anyone else. And you are going to stop treating me like a rebellious twelve-year-old who is about to have her virtue stolen. I'm twenty-six years old and quite capable of handling a man on my own. Now, what you *are* going to do is behave, because if you don't..." Annie paused and took a deep breath. "If you don't I'll—I'll—tell Mrs. Altero you hate her cooking." She would do no such thing, but it was the worst threat she could think of at the moment. In spite of Sal's macho posture, he had the kindest heart she'd ever known. He was the only one in the neighborhood who still allowed Mrs. Altero to use him as a guinea pig for her culinary catastrophes. Sal would rather suffer permanent indigestion than hurt her feelings.

"You wouldn't do that, Annie—" his smile was quizzical as he cocked his head to look at her "—would you?"

Smiling, Annie called his bluff, nodding slowly. "Now what's it going to be?" she asked, crossing her arms across her chest. "Are you going to behave or do I snitch to Mrs. Altero?"

"You're cruel, Annie," he complained, smiling in spite of himself. "And you drive a hard bargain."

"Remember what I said," she called as Sal clumped dejectedly down the stairs. "Behave yourself."

Why couldn't Annie understand he was just concerned about her? Hell, she was going out with some guy she didn't even know. A round of jealousy seized him.

What did this David guy know about Annie? Nothing. Sal knew her better than anyone. He'd seen her mischievous smile, the way her dark eyes lit up with wicked amusement when something tickled her, the way her eyes drooped when she was sleepy. He knew her every nuance, knew every little facet and characteristic of her personality.

After Tony's untimely death, it was only natural for him to step in to help Annie. She'd been left all alone. All she had was him and his mother and Aunt Florina. They'd taken her under their wing, drawing her into the fold of the family.

But Annie was far from being the helpless widow, Sal thought with a smile. She could hold her own with anyone—including him. Sal liked that. Annie didn't take any guff from anyone. She had character, integrity, and a feistiness about her that was very attractive. No wonder Tony had fallen in love with her. Sal's jaw tightened. Tony had been his best friend, but that didn't mean he approved of everything he'd done. Sal dragged a weary hand through his hair.

For two long years he'd hidden the truth from Annie, shielding her and protecting her, knowing that if she ever found out what really happened the night her husband was killed, she would be devastated. He could talk to her about anything—except that. It was bad enough that he had to live with it. He didn't want her to go through the same anguish. What was the point? Tony was dead, and nothing could bring him back. Annie's knowing how he died wouldn't change anything; all it would do was hurt her, and Sal would never intentionally do that. So he'd covered for his friend in death, just as he had in life. Sal always thought that someday he would tell her the truth, but someday never came, so he carried the burden alone, knowing he would do anything to protect her.

Sal sighed. He'd been so patient, biding his time, trying to ease Annie over the pain of Tony's death. He'd never failed at anything, but over the past two years he failed to stop his growing affection for Annie.

He'd dated lots of women, trying to blot out the feelings he had for her, but it didn't work. He would go out with a woman once or twice, and then move on. It wasn't fair to encourage anyone when he knew he couldn't return their affection. The only woman he wanted was . . . Annie.

Sometimes at night, he would lie in bed thinking about her, wanting her so badly that he couldn't sleep. He could not possibly tell her how he felt, so he'd carefully kept a veil on his emotions. She was his best friend's widow, for God's sake!

He knew eventually she would start dating again, but he hadn't expected it to happen so suddenly. An unexpected wave of possessiveness and protectiveness washed over him and he shook his head.

What the hell was he going to do? Guilt and jealousy warred within him. If he didn't do something—and quickly—she would be waltzing out into the night with a man neither of them knew a thing about. He couldn't—wouldn't—let that happen. He had to find some way to discourage her, as well as some way to keep an eye on this guy and his intentions. What was he going to do?

"Sal?" Annie called from the top of the stairs. Her soft voice jolted him back to reality. "Is something wrong? Why are you just standing at the bottom of the stairs?'' Maybe he really was ill, she thought in alarm. That would certainly explain his bizarre behavior.

"I was just thinking," Sal said, turning to look at her. His breath withered in his throat. "Annie," he breathed softly, stunned. Although petite in stature, Annie was exquisitely proportioned. She had on a slinky, black something-or-other that bared her arms and shoulders and draped softly over her full breasts, falling to gently swirling pleats just above her knees. She also wore high-heeled sandals that emphasized the feminine shape of her legs. Even in her high heels, she barely reached his shoulders. She was so beautiful, she almost took his breath away.

Recovering from his shock, Sal frowned. "Where did you get that dress?" he demanded, resisting the urge to cover her up with something. She was all dressed up to go out with some other guy!

"It looks terrible, doesn't it?" she said softly, tears quickly filling her eyes. "I knew I shouldn't have bought—"

"No, no, no," he quickly assured her, taking her hand the way he had done thousands of times. He was achingly familiar with her, but never more aware of her femininity than at this moment. "It looks...it looks—" Sal swallowed hard "—it looks beautiful." His eyes met hers and he gently lifted his finger to wipe away a tear that had slipped down her cheek. He never wanted Annie to cry again. "Don't cry, you look beautiful."

"Do you really think so?" she asked, her eyes sparkling with pleasure. She twirled on the steps, and Sal's muscles tightened as her soft, silky skirt flared out, giving him a first-class view of her legs. The corners of his mouth turned down.

"Really," he said grumpily, taking her hand and leading her down the stairs. David was sitting on the couch, flipping through a magazine. His eyes lit up when he saw Annie. Sal watched David carefully, not liking the sudden gleam in the man's eyes. He looked like a starving Doberman who had just gotten his first glimpse of a rare filet.

"Don't you look wonderful," David commented, causing Sal to scowl furiously. "If you're ready, Ann, we'd better get going. I've made reservations at Fairchilds, and if we're late, they won't hold our table." He looked Sal up and down, instantly dismissing him. "If you'll excuse us."

"Why?" Sal growled. "What are you planning on doing?"

"Sal!" Annie shot him a warning look.

Shaking his head, Sal went to the closet and extracted Annie's raincoat. "We don't want you to catch cold," he explained helpfully, draping the garment over Annie's shoulders and firmly snapping it closed all the way up to her chin.

"Sal," she began ominously, slapping his hands away and shrugging out of her rain gear. She clenched her teeth together so tightly they hurt. "It's the middle of June. It's eighty degrees outside and there's not a chance in hell of me—"

"Don't swear, Ann Marie," Sal scolded, and Annie rolled her eyes, taking a deep breath. It was one thing for Sal to be concerned about her reentry into society, but quite another for him to embarrass her to death. She'd had just about enough of his overprotective attitude.

"I don't need my raincoat," she persisted, her dark eyes flashing fire. "And I'm *not* going to catch cold. Now, Sal, I'm sure you have plans tonight, *with Mrs. Altero*," she said, grimly reminding him of her threat. "So if you don't mind, David and I will just run along." She tried to push past him, but Sal didn't budge.

"Will you go away?" she whispered under her breath. "David and I will be perfectly fine, won't we?" She turned to David, who grinned.

"Don't you worry, Sal, ole boy," David quipped, reaching out to slap Sal soundly on the shoulder. "Our Annie here will be in good hands," David assured him with a wink, causing Sal to take a threatening step closer. "*Very* good hands."

"You'd better just watch where you put those hands," Sal warned, wondering where this fool got this *our* Annie stuff from.

"Good night, Sal," Annie said firmly. "I'll talk to you tomorrow."

Chapter Three

He really hadn't intended to follow them, Sal thought as he glanced around Fairchilds. What he wanted to do was make sure David was treating Annie right. He strode to the bar and ordered a beer. Fairchilds was located in one of the priciest sections of town, and was just the place for a quiet seduction, Sal thought sourly.

The dimly lit bar was set off to one side of the restaurant, giving him a prime view of not only the doorway but the entire restaurant. The walls were decorated in heavy silk paper in shades of muted gray and beige. The carpeting was so thick, one could probably lose their shoes in it. The small, intimate tables were adorned with white linen cloths and tiny sprays of white roses in cut-crystal vases. Waiters dressed in tuxedos moved silently about, catering to the every whim of the well-heeled patrons, as a string quartet quietly filled the air with the sounds of soft, romantic tunes.

A wall of mirrors faced the bar. From his perch, he could see the entire restaurant, yet not be seen. Lifting his beer to his lips, Sal widened his eyes and almost choked as he spotted David and Annie sitting at a quiet table in the corner.

David must have taken Annie to his apartment! The kilt was gone, replaced by an obviously expensive gray pinstripe suit, white oxford-cloth shirt and silk foulard tie. Sal grimaced as his gaze shifted to Annie. She looked rather pale to him, except for the twin spots of color on her cheeks. He looked at her carefully, resisting the urge to dust her for fingerprints. If Dancing David had laid a hand on Annie, he would wring his skinny little neck.

Turning his back to them, Sal watched them in the mirror, feeling his guts twist as David leaned close to Annie. If the man was hard-of-hearing, why didn't he get a hearing aid? Sal wondered in disgust.

"Really, Ann," David droned on, oblivious to the glazed expression on her face. "I don't know what I would have done without my bonds, what with the current stock crisis and all. But at least I've still got my Remingtons." He sighed heavily. "Not that I'd ever sell them, mind you. They are after all much more than investments; they're works of art. Now, really, Ann, I think you should reconsider my proposition. A woman like you, all alone with no one to look after you, running a store in that neighborhood. It's a disgrace, I tell you. And I'm sure I could get you a good price for the deli...."

With sinking spirits, Annie forced herself to tune David out. She should have known this was a mistake. This was the third time—at least—since they'd arrived at Fairchilds that David had brought up the fact that she was a woman living alone.

Poor Annie, the little widow woman. She sighed in annoyance. What was it all of a sudden? First Sal. Now David had insisted on treating her as if she were Heidi the little goat girl, instead of a grown woman capable of handling her own life.

She hadn't really wanted to start dating again, anyway, Annie realized, feeling unaccountably awkward and uncomfortable. Even though David hadn't really done anything—except manage to touch her whenever the opportunity arose—she wished she was anywhere but here—with him.

She'd forgotten how strained conversation could be with a man you barely knew. They had already covered the weather, David's investments, David's art, and now, David's views regarding the subject of safety in her life—a subject she was not in the least bit interested in pursuing. Resentment bubbled over at David's attitude. The way he was talking, he made her feel as if she lived in a cardboard shack in the very worst part of town.

He would never understand why she still chose to live in the old neighborhood. To her, Little Italy was home. In fact, she couldn't imagine living anywhere else. Ever. It was a small community where everyone still knew everyone else, more like an extended family. But she didn't expect David to understand. They came from totally different worlds.

"Please," she finally said, pleating her linen napkin with a vengeance to air her sudden frustration. "I'm perfectly happy with my life and my home."

"Yes, I know, Ann. But you must realize the neighborhood is no longer the safe haven it once was. Surely you're aware that the area surrounding Little Italy is declining. You'd be much safer—"

Annie held up her hand. She didn't want to hear another word. "David, please." She rubbed a throbbing spot between her brows. David's cologne was cloyingly sweet, almost nauseating. Nothing like Sal's musky, male scent. She hadn't stopped thinking about him. The expression on Sal's face as she'd waltzed out the door on David's arm had haunted her most of the evening. He'd looked so perplexed, it filled her with a sad sense of longing that closed around her heart like a fist.

Just because it was time for her to get on with her life was no reason to deliberately hurt Sal. He'd been too good to her for that. He was just upset about her date with David, she assured herself. It would take some time for Sal to get used to the idea. Annie had to admit it looked as if it were going to take some time for her to get used to the idea of dating, as well.

"I'm sorry." David smiled and patted her hand. "I don't mean to nag. It's just that I'm concerned about your welfare."

"Well, you needn't be," she assured him, forcing herself to be polite. "As long as Sal's around, I'm perfectly safe." Annie smiled, realizing how true the statement was. He was the whole reason for this dating ritual, to begin with. That was the problem: Sal *was* always around, always there for her to lean on. She'd grown too dependent on him, knowing no matter what, he would be there. It was time she learned to depend on herself. Leaning on Sal had become an expensive habit Annie knew she could no longer afford—for his sake as well as her own.

But this wasn't quite how she expected her first date to be. She thought it would be fun and light, not a chore with forced conversation, tense silences and awkward smiles. She didn't know why, but she was acutely uncomfortable with David. Perhaps it was just that she was used to Sal's company. With him, conversation just flowed, with no awkward moments or long, tense silences. She felt comfortable with him. Maybe she was spoiled, Annie mused. It had been a long, long time since she'd felt as if she had to impress someone, and for some reason she had the feeling David was waiting to be impressed.

She knew it wasn't right or fair to compare David to Sal, but she couldn't seem to prevent herself. Sal was such fun, no matter what they did, whether it was going for a walk in Peanut Park or having Sunday dinner at his mother's, they had fun. She was comfortable with him, and never felt as if she had to put on airs, or pretend to be someone she wasn't.

But Sal was just a friend, she reminded herself. *Tony's best friend.* Yet, earlier this evening, before David had arrived, the feelings she'd felt for Sal had nothing to do with friendship, but a whole lot to do with male-female relationships.

"Yes, dear, but . . ."

Annie blinked, realizing she'd drifted off into her own thoughts again and wasn't listening to one word her date said.

"I'm sorry, David," she said, forcing a smile she didn't feel. The throbbing in her head was getting worse. "What were you saying?"

A frown seemed permanently etched between his bushy blond brows. "Yes, well, I was saying I can't believe that man actually wears his weapon everywhere he goes. It's positively indecent. He struts about like some ancient barbarian."

Annie bit back a smile. There was no doubt who "that man" was, but boy, would she love to see Sal's expression if he could hear David's rather vivid description of him. "Ancient barbarian," indeed! A sense of loyalty caused her skin to prickle. David might not like Sal, but that was certainly no reason for him to be critical.

"David," she said carefully, trying to hide her annoyance. "Sal's a cop. He doesn't carry his gun just for show. He has a very dangerous job."

"'Dangerous,'" David sniffed, lifting his drink to his lips. "How quaint."

Annie lifted her head to issue an angry retort. The breath withered in her throat as she saw a large male presence moving toward them. *Sal.* Oh, Lord, what was he doing here? She couldn't help the rush of relief that washed over her.

"Uh-oh," David said ominously, catching sight of Sal. "Looks like we have company." He nodded in Sal's direction, and Annie felt her heart take flight.

She wished she didn't feel quite so happy, or relieved, to see him.

David's eyes flicked over Sal dismissively, as if he were something unpleasant crawling toward them across the plush carpet.

She watched Sal approach, looking as if he owned the world. David was right about one thing: Sal *did* strut about and he *did* remind of her of an old-fashioned man from days gone by. She smiled in pleasure. Not a barbarian exactly, but more like a sexy pirate, or a renegade. With his dark olive complexion, his glittering, intense eyes and self-assured style, Sal could have stepped right out of the pages of an eighteenth-century historical novel. No wonder women found him so attractive, she thought, feeling her own response to him.

She glanced at David, noting the tense look on his face. Oh, Lord. She hoped they didn't create a scene. She could handle this, couldn't she? Looking at David again, she wasn't so sure.

"David," Annie began, sensing a problem.

"Please." David covered her hand and flashed her a toothy smile. "Let me take care of this," he said confidently.

Sal stopped just inches from their table, an engaging smile on his face and a bottle of wine in his hands. Annie tried hard to drag up some annoyance to replace the relief she felt as she gently retrieved her hand from David's. Sal had no right to follow her, but she'd never been so happy to see anyone in her life, and her smile showed it.

"Well, well, well," Sal commented, looking directly at Annie and deliberately ignoring David. "Fancy meeting you here."

"Yes," David murmured none too graciously. "*Quite* a coincidence."

"What are you doing here?" Annie asked with a calmness she didn't feel. She should be furious that he had followed her, but what she was feeling right now was simply gratitude.

Sal grinned. "I was thirsty," he lied, handing a bottle of wine to the hovering waiter and taking the chair he offered.

"Thirsty," David repeated in disdain, glancing suspiciously at the bottle the waiter was now opening. "Dom Perignon. I didn't think a civil servant could afford such luxuries."

Annie's glance went from David to Sal. David had better be careful; this servant didn't look too civil to her at the moment.

"Well, Davey," Sal drawled, his eyes twinkling with mischief. "You'd be surprised at our resources." Wait until ole Davey found out he had charged the wine to Davey's tab!

"No doubt." David reached out and covered Annie's hand with his again. Sal's gaze followed his movement, and Annie noted the sudden possessive gleam in his eye. His face grew tight, angry. She had a feeling David was deliberately trying to annoy Sal, and if the look on Sal's face was any indication, he was doing a good job.

Annie was tempted to pull her hand free of David's. His touch was cold and clammy, but to yank her hand away would have been rude. She didn't like being a pawn for anyone, and David's actions seemed deliberate. Her stomach tightened. She'd always hated verbal confrontations, and she had a feeling she was about to be drawn right smack dab into the middle of one.

"What brings you to this part of town?" David inquired. "This hardly seems like the type of place someone like *you* would frequent."

"David!" Annie turned to him in alarm. She might be furious at Sal for following her, but that was between her and Sal. It didn't give David the right to be rude. Sal was only looking out for her, only trying to protect her. So how could she be angry?

"Someone like me?" Sal repeated, a small smile on his face. The only hint of his annoyance was the lowered tone of his voice. "And what type of *someone* am I?"

Oh, Lord, Annie thought, rolling her eyes toward the heavens. If David had as much sense as money, he would lighten up. Sal wasn't the type of man to be pushed around or insulted, by anyone.

David smiled benignly, tightening his grip on Annie's hand. "Oh, you know," he said vaguely, taking a menu from the still-hovering waiter and making a great show of handing one to Annie. She retrieved her hand from his and stared at her menu, not seeing a word of it.

She had no idea what David and Sal thought they were accomplishing, other than annoying her. This wasn't just pleasant social banter any longer; this was some kind of traditional macho, possessive ritual, and apparently *she* was the possession. Evidently it hadn't occurred to either man that neither had a right to be possessive about her or her company.

"Will there be three for dinner?" the waiter inquired politely.

"No," David said firmly.

"Yes," Sal corrected smoothly, taking the other menu out of the waiter's hand before he had a chance to hand it to David. Sighing, Annie shared her menu with David, ignoring his closeness as he dipped his head to read the evening's selections. His cologne infiltrated her breathing space. Unconsciously, she raised a hand to rub her forehead.

"Got a headache, Annie?" Sal inquired softly, ignoring David who looked up in surprise. She always rubbed her forehead in that circling motion whenever she had a headache. It was just one of a thousand endearing things he knew about Annie.

"No doubt," David said, giving Sal a look that clearly said *he* was the reason for Annie's sudden headache.

"Yes. But I can't imagine why," she added dryly, looking from one man to the other with barely disguised irritation. She was not going to just sit here while these two did whatever it was they thought they were doing.

"Excuse me," Annie said, standing up and scooping her purse from the table. "I think I'll go take some aspirin." She hoped that whatever was going on would be settled by the time she returned.

Both men stood up, almost knocking their chairs over in an effort to beat each other to their feet.

Shaking her head in disgust, Annie headed for the ladies' room.

"Look, Sal," David said. "Let's put our cards on the table, shall we? Ann's told me all about you. I can understand how you might feel a certain...obligation to her and all, but you aren't her keeper."

Sal's jaw tightened, and he looked at David darkly. "What I am to Annie," he said quietly, "is really none of your business."

"On the contrary," David replied smoothly. "It *is* my business. She's with *me* tonight. Let's face it, Ann's a beautiful woman. She's been without a man for two long, lonely years."

"So?" Sal's expression turned to stone.

"So..." David shrugged, grinning broadly. "Come on, Sal, we both know a woman like Ann, all alone without a man for so long..." David winked boldly. "You understand, sport, don't you?"

Sal understood, all too clearly. He felt his temper boil over as all his protective and possessive instincts came to light. It took a supreme effort for him not to rearrange David's face.

"You see," David went on, oblivious to the danger glinting in Sal's stormy eyes, "*I know exactly what Ann needs and wants.* And I'm the kind of man who *always* gives a lady what she wants." David winked again and Sal shot to his feet. "If you know what I mean."

"If you lay a hand on her I swear I'll—"

"Sal!" Shocked, Annie grabbed his arm, dismayed at his behavior. "What on earth is wrong with you?"

She looked from David to Sal in total confusion. "With both of you?"

The two men glared at each other, neither of them admitting or acknowledging what the problem was.

"Look, I've had just about enough of this," Annie warned. "You're both acting like children, and I'm tired of it." She turned on Sal, deciding to tackle one problem at a time. "You had no right to follow me," she scolded, growing furious at David's smug grin. "And you," she snapped, whirling on David, "had no right to be so rude. Sal is a friend of mine, and I expect you to keep a civil tongue." David's smile slid off his face. Annie drew herself up and took a deep breath. "Now we can either all have a nice dinner, together, or—" she swept them both with a glare "—or I'm going home. *Alone.* Now what is it going to be?" She looked at Sal, whose lips tightened into a grim line.

If Annie thought he was going to leave her alone with this loose-lipped lech she was in for a rude surprise. He wasn't budging until he was certain she was safe and sound, and if that meant crawling in Dancing David's pocket for the rest of the evening, that's exactly what he intended to do.

Sal looked at David. Unless they made some attempt at peace, Annie would leave, and he knew he would never convince her that David was the wrong man for her. She would just accuse him of being jealous and overprotective. Hell, he *was* jealous and overprotective. But he had to do something to salvage the situation.

Sal extended his hand to David. He would make peace, for Annie's sake.

David took it giving Sal a measured look. "As long as we understand each other," he said coldly.

"Oh, we do," Sal said, matching David stare for stare. "Believe me, I understand you perfectly."

"Good. Shall we order?" Annie asked, taking her seat and breathing a sigh of relief. Hopefully things would return to normal. She wasn't certain how normal three on a date was, but she was going to do her part.

Dinner was a silent, strained affair. Annie felt David's and Sal's eyes on her during the whole meal, making her increasingly uncomfortable. Her appetite disappeared and her headache worsened. She should have known this was a mistake. She'd had more fun going to the movies with Mr. Finucci, even if he did fall asleep on her shoulder and snore in her ear.

Once the table was cleared and coffee poured, Annie tried to mentally prepare herself for the next round between the men. The tension was thick enough to cut with an ax. All she wanted to do was go home and crawl into bed and pretend this evening had never happened.

"Ann," David said, deliberately ignoring Sal. "Would you care to dance? They have a wonderful combo—"

"Dancing is out of the question," Sal responded before she had a chance to open her mouth. She turned to him with a scowl and he grinned, obviously enjoying himself. "Annie has two left feet," he confided to David.

"Sal," Annie began ominously. Heaving an exasperated sigh, David stood up and threw his napkin on the table. Oh, Lord, they were at it again.

"David, please?" she implored, reaching out for his jacket.

"Let me handle this," David said, brushing off her arm. "Now see here, Sal ole boy. I think you're carrying this protectiveness a bit too far. Ann's a big girl, and she certainly doesn't need your permission to dance with me *or* go out with me. I thought we'd settled all this."

"Oh, it's settled, all right," Sal said calmly, standing up and wedging himself between David and Annie.

"Sal," Annie warned, but he ignored her. She slowly stood up, staring at Sal intensely. "David, would you please excuse us for a moment?"

"Yes, David," Sal added, his eyes twinkling mischievously. "Why don't you go... powder your nose, or something."

Pivoting on his heel, David gave Sal a dark look before storming off.

"Are you crazy?" Annie cried, giving Sal a whack on the arm. "What has gotten into you tonight? What are you doing here?"

"I told you, I was thirsty," he lied, trying not to grin at her harassed expression.

"Sal." Her eyes darkened.

They glared at one another for a long, silent moment and finally Sal flashed her a wicked grin. "Are you mad, Annie?"

"Mad!" Annie yelled, ignoring the startled look of the waiter who was hovering close by. She glared up into Sal's amused face, deliberately lowering her voice. "Would you care to explain to me why I'm dragging a deranged detective around with me? This is supposed to be a date for two, Sal, not three!"

"Are you saying you don't want me here?" he asked, trying to look properly hurt. Her anger softened.

"I've got a good mind to call your mother and tell her what you've been doing," Annie complained, wondering what she was going to do with him.

"It's your own fault," Sal accused, trying without success to banish a wicked grin.

"My fault?" Annie said angrily, giving him another whack. "Why is it my fault that *you*'re behaving like a lunatic?"

A waiter approached, clutching his hands to his chest in dismay. "Please, please, *please*!" he whispered. "We're not accustomed to scenes here. You must lower your voices or I'll have to ask you to leave. You're disturbing the other diners." He glanced quickly around the room, wringing his hands.

"I'm sorry," Annie said contritely, glaring at Sal and feeling acute embarrassment.

"If you would have let me check this guy out, none of this would have happened," Sal murmured, leaning close so only she could hear him. "I don't know a thing about this guy, and what I do know, I don't like."

"Sal, you don't have to like him," she defended hotly. "You're not dating him, *I* am."

Annie stared at him, not sure whether she should be touched by his concern or furious over his behavior. What on earth was she going to do with him?

Why was he acting like this? For a moment she almost believed he *was* jealous. But Annie quickly dismissed the idea. Sal, jealous? The idea was almost ludicrous.

She'd seen the parade of women that filtered in and out of his life. He wasn't known as "Smooth, Suave Sal" for nothing. The women Sal chose to spend his time with usually bore little or no resemblance to her or her type.

No, the women Sal was attracted to were usually buxom blondes with names like Bambi, Bobbi, Wendi or Suzi. Most had an easier time putting on their lipstick than carrying on an intelligent conversation. So the idea that Sal was jealous was foolish. Overprotective, maybe, but jealous, no.

She knew exactly what Sal was—a man who loved women and his freedom, and not necessarily in that order. He wasn't about to settle down to domestic life, or be satisfied with just one woman when he could have them all....

Sal jealous of David? Annie shook her head. Sal behaving like some medieval knight? If she didn't know better, she would think he was trying to protect her virtue! Next he would probably order her a chastity belt!

"Sal, please go home?" She remembered to lower her voice as the waiter approached, followed by David, who looked mad enough to spit nickels. "Here comes David," Annie announced. "Now I want you to leave."

The waiter hovered closely, watching as Sal and David stood toe-to-toe, glaring at each other. "I'm sorry, Mr. Donaldson, but I'm afraid I'm going to have to ask you and your party to leave. This establishment is not accustomed to this type of behavior."

Annie dropped her head. Cow cakes! In all her life she'd never been thrown out of a restaurant.

"We were just leaving, anyway," David said, deliberately ignoring Sal. "It's getting rather late—"

"Must be all of nine-thirty," Sal quipped, and Annie shot him a fierce glance.

"Why don't I take you home, Ann?" David glanced at Sal. "We can do this again another night."

Don't bet your tassels on it, Sal thought, following David as he slid his arm around Annie and led her toward the door. Sal kept a respectable distance behind them, following David's zippy little import all the way to Annie's door.

Whistling softly, Sal stepped from his car and headed up the walk. He shrugged his jacket off and sat down on the steps. Annie was still sitting in the car with David. If David ever showed his face around Annie again, the man was far braver than Sal had given him credit for. But if he did, Sal intended to be right on his heels. Give the lady what she wants, indeed!

Sal was certain he could handle Dancing David, but Annie—now there was a problem. He had no doubt she was furious at him for his behavior. And, furious or not, he'd accomplished his mission. But how on earth was he ever going to explain his actions to Annie?

He didn't know, but he sure as hell was going to try.

Sal dragged a hand through his hair. Despite the fact that Annie was alone and free—physically, emotionally and legally—Sal knew what he was feeling wasn't right. She was his best friend's widow, for God's sake.

Sal stood as Annie climbed out of David's car. The moonlight danced off her delicate features, catching the gleam in her eye. A murderous gleam, Sal thought, watching her stomp up the stairs. He sure hoped he could talk his way out of this.

"Did you have a nice time?" he inquired by way of opening.

Annie stopped dead in front of him. "No, I did not," she snapped, wondering where he got his gall from.

"Are you mad at me, Annie?" he inquired again unnecessarily. She glared at him.

"Why on earth should I be mad?" Annie cried, trying without success not to raise her voice. "Just because you've ruined my date and my evening, not to mention the fact that you've insulted a very nice man for no apparent reason, now why would I be mad?"

Sal bent down and pressed his amused face close to hers. "I guess you *are* mad, huh?"

"Agguh!" Annie growled, stomping past him and on up the stairs. "I have never been so embarrassed in my life!" she fumed.

"Yes, you were; remember the time—" The look she flashed him stopped him cold. He decided to try a different tactic. "I could sure use a nightcap," he suggested as she pushed past him.

"I'll give you a nightcap," Annie muttered.

Sal dropped his hand to her arm and Annie came to an abrupt halt. For a moment she simply stared at his hand, stunned at the power of one small limb to evoke so many feelings.

She was absolutely furious at Sal, livid in fact. But the warmth swamping through her had nothing to do with her temper.

Annie blinked, her eyes assessing his hand. Sal had nice hands, she thought absently. Large and well formed, with a light dusting of dark, curly hair. It wasn't the appearance of his hand that was affecting her, but his . . . touch.

Stunned, Annie lifted her eyes to his. His were dark, unreadable. Sal fastened his gaze on her lips and Annie silently sucked in her breath as her pulse fluttered wildly.

"Annie?" Her name was a whispery sigh, floating away on the faint summer breeze. As if drawn by a magnet, Annie lifted her eyes, then slowly looked at the softness of his mouth. Fascinated by the sensuous fullness of his lips, Annie moistened her own parched lips, wondering why she was suddenly feeling so off kilter. It had to be her anger.

Sal stepped down one step, and Annie arched her neck to meet his gaze. She tried to take a step back, but he tightened his fingers on her arm, preventing her from moving.

Her senses grew acute in the encompassing darkness. She could hear every intake of her breath, raspy as it was. Annie could feel the faint breeze dance across her face, washing her in Sal's fragrant, familiar scent. She could see the uncertainty in his eyes as they found hers.

Something was happening between them, something she wasn't sure she could name. All she knew was that it was powerful... and frightening.

"Sal, I'd better go—"

"I'm sorry," he whispered, lifting a hand to brush a curl off her cheek. His touch burned her skin. "I'm sorry I ruined your evening," he lied, and Annie smiled glumly.

"No, you're not," she returned. Sal chuckled softly and took another step closer. Unconsciously Annie stepped back.

"You're right," he whispered. "I'm not sorry." Stunned, she looked up at him with wide, luminous eyes.

The urge to see if Annie tasted as sweet as she looked engulfed him. Sal didn't even try to hide his feelings. He wanted to kiss Annie, and he didn't know why. All he knew was that he'd never wanted anything more; and Sal Giordiano always got what he wanted.

"You did that on purpose, didn't you?" she asked.

"Did what?" he whispered, lifting one hand to cradle her cheek. His eyes held hers and Annie swallowed hard, trying to keep her thoughts on the problem at hand and not on Sal's closeness.

"Ruined... my date with... with..." She blinked slowly, trying to break the thread that seemed to be drawing her closer and closer to him. She'd always been emotional, but she'd never been irrational. She needed to take a deep breath, but somehow she couldn't find the strength, the pressure on her chest was so great. Finally, blessedly, her breath came, jostling through her rib cage. "My date with . . ."

"David," Sal supplied helpfully, and she nodded.

"Yes. D-David." Sal slowly slid his thumb across her bottom lip and Annie sucked in her breath. He was much too experienced not to recognize her response to him. Her quick intake of breath, the sudden expansion of her pupils, the simultaneous tightening of her body. Her full lips parted softly.

"Sal?" she whispered, her voice soft and raspy as she tried to make some sense of what was happening to her—to him—to them.

Sal held her in a tender embrace, his large hands gently cradling her face. Annie tried to retreat, but found her legs wouldn't move. Her heart slammed into her rib cage as she helplessly watched his lips slowly descend toward her.

Annie opened her mouth to protest. Sal's lips possessively claimed hers until her breath mingled with his. Reason fled as sensation after sensation stormed through her, awakening her slumbering senses.

Instinctively she slid her hands up his arms, feeling the taut strength of his muscles. She wrapped her arms around his neck, arching her body toward his, warming to his heat and seeking more. A wordless cry of desire echoed through her mind as Sal slid his hand down to her narrow waist, hauling her unsuspecting body close until she pressed against him from shoulder to knee.

Sal felt her soft, feminine curves mold gently to his masculine hardness. His mouth worked hers gently, seeking, exploring. A soft whimper escaped her parted lips as Sal's tongue gently tapped at the seam of her mouth. Shivers of delighted awareness chased each other up and down her spine. His body was like a lightning rod of heat, drawing her close.

A voice of protest echoed dully in the back of Annie's foggy brain, but she ignored it. She knew she shouldn't be kissing Sal—not like this. He was a friend. Just a friend. But Annie knew that somehow, someway, this kiss, the emotions that swept over her, were not the feelings evoked by just a friend. In one split second, Sal had changed from being her best friend, to something much, much more.

Sal slid his hand from her cheek to caress her neck. He pulled her closer, wanting to melt into her warmth and softness. Annie angled her head, following the movements of Sal's lips. Desire coiled inside her like a ribbon, causing her body to ache with forgotten need.

"Salvatore!" Mrs. Altero called from across the street, waving her hand. "There you are. Thank God. I've been looking all over for you." She hurried across the street, her plump body swaying from side to side.

Sal drew back and groaned softly. Of all the times for Mrs. Altero to chase him down. His eyes met Annie's and she stared at him in stupefied silence. Her mind was a muddled mess and Annie couldn't seem to untangle all the thoughts and emotions racing through her.

"Annie?" he whispered, his voice so reverent it made her legs weak.

Blinking slowly, she stepped back until her legs were pressed against the black wrought-iron railing of the steps. Her breaths were quick and short, her pulse zipping frantically through her veins.

Sal looked at her in confusion, just as stunned as she at the impact of their kiss. Sal had dated a lot of women, kissed a lot of women, but none had affected him as much as Annie's kiss.

He cocked his head and looked at her, seeing her through new eyes. She was no longer the widow of his partner, or just a good friend. She was a beautiful, desirable woman.

Annie continued to stare at Sal, confused and perplexed, knowing she wanted nothing more at the moment than to walk back into his arms and feel the warmth and comfort of his embrace—not only as a friend but as a lover. Annie sighed as a wave of guilt and confusion engulfed her. How, she wondered, had this happened?

"Salvatore! Salvatore!" Mrs. Altero hurried across the street, puffing hard. She placed a hand to her chest and took a deep breath. "Thank God." Mrs. Altero paused and inhaled deeply again. "We've been looking all over for you. And you, too, Annie," the older woman added.

"I'm sorry I couldn't make dinner tonight," Sal said sheepishly, his eyes never leaving Annie's. "But Annie and I—"

"No, no, no, that's not why I was looking for you."
Mrs. Altero paused to take another deep breath.
"Salvatore. It was awful. The store—the deli—
Someone broke in tonight."

Chapter Four

What!'' Sal and Annie caroled in unison.

"What do you mean, someone broke into the deli?'' Sal's voice was deadly quiet. Momentarily bewildered, Annie stared blankly at Mrs. Altero. This was ridiculous. It had to be a mistake. Who would want to break into her little deli? For what? She never kept more than fifty dollars in cash.

"It was awful, Salvatore,'' Mrs. Altero wailed, wringing her plump hands together. "They broke the glass windows—and we couldn't find you, or Annie—and—'' Annie had heard enough. She bolted down the stairs, nearly trampling Mrs. Altero in the rush. Sal grabbed her arm and hung on.

"Wait, Annie,'' Sal ordered, reining her in close to him. He didn't want her going off without him, at least not until he heard the rest of this.

"But the deli,'' she protested, struggling to get free.

"Let's hear what happened first." He dropped his arm around her shoulders, holding her in place, and Annie had no choice but to wait.

"Mrs. Altero, take a deep breath and tell me exactly what happened," Sal ordered.

Doing as she was told, Mrs. Altero attempted to compose herself. "Salvatore, my granddaughter and I were going down to Letza's for Italian ice. When we passed the deli I noticed something funny. The lights were on." She turned to Annie. "I know you're never open on Saturday nights, so we crossed the street, and that's when I noticed—" Mrs. Altero stopped and clutched her chest. "It was awful. The window was shattered. There was glass everywhere. I was going to go in—"

"You didn't, did you?" Sal interrupted, his voice low and commanding. Mrs. Altero shook her head.

"No, Salvatore, I remember what you always told us. I didn't go in. No, sir." She shook her gray head. "I came home and called the police station just like you instructed, and then I called the board-up company. I tried to find you, but . . ."

He patted her shoulder and smiled. "You did fine, Mrs. Altero. Just fine. Thank you."

"Sal, please, I want to see what happened." Annie's voice shook and she turned to Sal with stricken eyes. This had to be a bad dream. Who would want to break into her store? For what?

"Come on, Annie." He led her down the stairs and around the corner to the deli. Annie's eyes widened and her mouth fell open.

"Oh, Sal." Her hand flew to her mouth as tears filled her eyes. The plate-glass window that fronted the store was boarded up; glass still littered the sidewalk. The front door had a large gaping hole in it.

"God," Sal whispered, tightening his arm around Annie's shoulders. He looked down at her. "Hey, are you all right?"

Annie raised her eyes to his and his heart constricted. "Sal, who would do something like this?" she whispered in fear, trembling uncontrollably.

He shook his head and drew her closer to him. "I don't know, honey, but I sure as hell am going to find out. Do you have your keys? I want to go in and take a look around."

Blinking away tears, Annie searched through her evening bag and handed Sal the keys. She clutched the back of his suit jacket as he opened the door and flipped on the lights.

"Oh, my God!" Annie's hand flew to her mouth. The store had been ransacked, not a shelf or a counter had been left untouched. While she catered to the neighborhood's needs, stocking special Italian items such as imported olive oils and tomatoes, she also carried a little bit of everything from soap to soup to laundry detergent.

Her eyes traveled slowly around the room. Every single display case and rack had been overturned. Boxes had been ripped open and dumped all over the wooden floor, cans and bottles had been smashed against the walls and left to drip sticky messes. The glass deli case had been shattered and emptied. Broken glass was spilled all over everything, spoiling all of her imported cheeses and meats. The old-fashioned cash register that sat on the waist-high counter was open and empty. The entire deli was a disaster.

"My God!" Annie whimpered, clutching Sal's arm. "They've ruined me."

"I want to call the station." Sal stripped off his jacket and slung it over his shoulder. "Don't touch anything, Annie," he ordered as she wandered around helplessly, sidestepping broken glass and puddles.

Numb, she walked up and down the aisles, trying to understand what had happened, and why. Who could do this, but more important, why? There was a large all-night market not two blocks away. Surely they had much more to offer than a small, neighborhood deli.

The deli had been her haven, her security, the one thing she had left after Tony died. Knowing someone had done this deliberately caused a shiver of terror to wash over her. She'd never felt so violated before.

Annie wandered around helplessly, nearly stumbling over a picture that had been hanging on the wall behind the counter. Without thinking, she bent over and picked it up. It was a picture of her, Tony and Sal that had been taken shortly before Tony died. The glass was shattered, the frame bent.

Unexpected tears filled her eyes and she clutched the photo to her heart. She felt so alone. And so frightened. How could someone do this to her?

"Annie?" Sal's voice was gentle as he pried the picture loose from her arms and set it on the counter. "I talked to the station. They've already been here to dust for prints. Their guess is it was an amateur, judging from the entry. But we'll need you to take an inventory and fill out a report as to what's missing. Do you think you can do that?'' He dropped his hands to her shoulders and looked at her intently. Her face was white as a sheet, her eyes glistening with tears.

"Sal, why?" She raised stricken eyes to his. He didn't know who had done this, or why. But he sure as hell was going to find out. He'd only seen her look like this once, and he'd vowed then she would never look that sad, that alone, that vulnerable again. Swearing softly, he hauled her into his arms.

Great racking sobs shook Annie's body, and she held on to Sal tightly. Stroking her hair, Sal let her cry until her tears subsided.

Sniffling, Annie drew back and took the handkerchief Sal offered, giving him a tremulous smile. What would she have done without him tonight? Or for the past two years? He was her knight in shining armor. Her eyes filled again and a soft cry escaped her. Sal quietly gathered her into his arms again. She was so grateful he was here by her side. She slid her arms around his waist and buried her face in his shirt.

"Annie?" He kept his arms around her, holding her close, enjoying the warmth and comfort of her. "Do you think you're up to taking inventory? I'll help."

Nodding, Annie blinked away her tears, lifting her tearstained face to his. Looking into his eyes, she was vividly reminded of the kiss they'd shared just moments ago. His mouth had been so soft, so sweet, his arms so comforting. It seemed like a lifetime ago. She had been trying so hard not to need him, but until this moment, she'd never realized just how much she really *did* need him. Annie pulled out of his arms.

"I'll have to go home and change. I can't take inventory until I clean this place up." She shrugged. "I don't know what's here or what's missing." She glanced around again and shivered suddenly.

"Come on," Sal said, draping an arm around her shoulders. "I'll go with you."

"You don't have to do that," she murmured, knowing she wanted nothing more than for Sal to stay with her, the closer the better. At least until this sudden attack of fear subsided.

"I know I don't have to," Sal said gently, brushing her hair off her face. "But I want to. Don't worry, we'll have this place cleaned up in time for you to open in the morning. Let's go get you changed and I'll call my mother and aunt and tell them what happened." Sal led her out the door, carefully locking it behind them. They walked back to Annie's house, and for the first time since she'd lived in the neighborhood, for the first time in her life, Annie realized she was frightened.

"What's wrong?" Sal asked as she inched closer to him, clutching his jacket as they walked.

"I'm scared," she whispered, scanning the darkened street. "I never thought I'd ever say that. I've lived in this neighborhood my whole life, walked up and down these streets on hundreds of nights without ever being afraid, but now—" She glanced up at him. "I never thought I'd be scared," she whispered, "but I am."

He tightened his arm around her as she hurried up the stairs of her house and opened the door. Slamming it shut soundly behind her, Annie took a deep breath when she realized her home was safe and sound. It was an old brownstone that she'd lovingly restored after her husband's death. Tonight it seemed even more warm and welcoming. Tonight it seemed— safe.

"I know how you feel," Sal said quietly, his eyes pinning hers. "But I'm here, Annie. You don't have to be afraid of anything, ever."

His words were reassuring. But she knew Sal wouldn't always be there for her. The thought brought a round of sadness. She thought that was what she wanted—not to be a burden to him anymore, to let him go and lead her own life and let him lead his. But now, the prospect of not having Sal around anymore terrified her, not just because of the burglary, but for reasons far more personal. Her gaze dropped to his lips, and she couldn't help remembering the touch and taste of Sal's mouth on hers. She suddenly felt like crying again.

"I'd better go change," she said hesitantly, glancing up the long oak stairway that led to her bedroom.

"Want me to come upstairs?" Sal asked, sensing her fear.

"I feel like a baby," she confessed, trying to smile as he took her hand and led her up the stairs. "It's just . . . I feel so . . . spooked," she said, unable to find a better word to describe what she was feeling.

"I know, honey. But you'll get over it, I promise." Sal waited right outside Annie's bedroom door while she changed, using the hall phone to call his mom and aunt to let them know what had happened.

His mother and his aunt worked for Annie part-time, and he knew if he didn't tell them, someone from the neighborhood would, and he didn't want them to worry. Everyone knew everything about everybody in the neighborhood. Word of the burglary would spread fast, and hopefully someone would remember something—anything—that would give him a clue as to who had done this. He surely hoped so. He couldn't remember ever wanting anyone as badly as he wanted the people responsible for doing this to Annie.

Once changed, Annie let Sal take her back to the deli where they set about cleaning up the place. After stripping off his suit jacket, Sal rolled up his sleeves and got to work.

"I'll start in this aisle," Sal instructed. "You start on the next. That way we can see each other." He smiled as Annie hesitantly let go of his hand. Despite the heat, Annie had thrown on a pair of old faded jeans and a short-sleeved sweater. She was cold, so cold, and she couldn't stop shivering.

"Sal," she asked after a few moments. "Why would anyone want to rob the deli? I mean, what could they possibly want?"

It was a question he'd been asking himself since they'd walked in. It didn't make sense. From the quick appraisal he had done, he really couldn't see anything missing. The place was wrecked, but whoever was responsible didn't seem to have been interested in anything other than the cash.

"I don't know, Annie. I just don't know."

"Sal, look at this." Annie handed Sal two empty candy wrappers she'd found on the floor. "What do you make of this?"

He frowned. "A hungry burglar?" he quipped, examining the wrappers carefully. Everything indicated this was the work of amateurs. *Stupid* amateurs, if they'd stopped to sample the merchandise. He sifted through the debris, looking for a plastic bag to put the evidence in.

A loud rapping on the door caused Annie to scream. She bolted straight into Sal's arms.

"Easy, Annie," he soothed, tightening his arms around her trembling body. He glanced over his shoulder and smiled. "It's only my mother and Auntie Florina." Embarrassed, Annie pulled out of his embrace.

Sal crossed the room with Annie right on his heels. He pulled open the door and grabbed both ladies up in a bear hug. "Ma! Auntie Florina!"

Rosina and Florina were twins. Everything about them was identical, from their neatly tucked silver buns to their somber black dresses, dark cotton stockings and low-heeled, sensible shoes. Each clutched a double-handled black pocketbook as if it contained her entire life savings. The only difference between the two was Florina's glasses—and her tongue. Florina was three minutes older and three times more vocal than her rather shy, demure twin.

"Who could do this, Salvatore?" his mother asked, surveying the deli with wide, frightened eyes.

"Punks!" Florina raged, shaking a fist in the air. "Annie, I brought you something." Florina stepped over the debris, patting Annie's hand reassuringly. "You take this," she ordered, handing Annie a baseball bat. "Anyone come into the store, you bop 'em with this. That will teach them."

"No, Auntie Florina," Sal admonished, banishing a smile and gingerly taking the weapon from her and leaning it against the wall. "That's a good way for Annie to get hurt. Let us handle it."

"Oh, Salvatore, if only Papa were alive," his mother said wistfully, dabbing at her eyes. "He would know what to do, how to handle this."

"Papa knew how to handle everything," Florina added. "Like our Salvatore, here. Right, sister?"

"Right." Rosina nodded. "My son, he's such a good boy," she told Annie, who smiled. Sal was hardly a boy. He was a man, all man, as she'd discovered tonight. But Florina was right. Sal *could* handle everything. Annie had never felt so grateful for his company or comfort.

"Come on, sister," Florina instructed, heading toward the back room. "Let's get our aprons and clean up this mess."

Annie knew it was useless to argue with them. She needed their help, and to refuse their offer would be an insult. Ever since Tony died—no, even before—they'd been so good to her. They'd taken her under their wing and been the family she didn't have. Annie couldn't love the twins any more if they *were* family.

"Sal," Annie said quietly, watching as he righted a small display stand. "Thank you."

He looked up at her in surprise. "For what?"

"For everything." Her eyes met his, and she quickly looked away. When Sal looked at her she felt her pulse pound recklessly. She could no longer look at Sal as just a friend, but had to see him as a man. A deliciously desirable, handsome man. Annie knew there was no place in her life—or his—for such feelings. He was just a friend. And she was just his obligation, she reflected sadly. In order to quell her disturbing thoughts, Annie grabbed a broom and began sweeping up a pile of loose pasta scattered along the floor.

"Salvatore," his mother whispered, coming up behind him so Annie wouldn't hear. "Florina and I—we're worried."

Sal straightened. "Ma, don't worry," he said, patting her shoulder. "It's over now. We'll have this place cleaned up in no time."

His mother shook her head. "It's not that," she said with a worried frown.

"What, then?"

Rosina and Florina exchanged glances. They said more with one look than most people said with a thousand words. Long ago Sal had learned to trust their intuition.

"There's this man," his mother began, glancing at Annie cautiously. She was busily sweeping, not paying the least bit of attention to them.

Florina grabbed Sal's arms and steered him around. "Salvatore. We didn't want to bother you, but..." Her voice trailed off and she glanced at her sister.

Sal looked from one to the other. "Ma, Auntie Florina, what is it? What man?" If there was some-

thing suspicious going on, he wanted to know about
it.

"Salvatore," his mother began. "This stranger, he's
been coming around and—"

"What stranger?" Sal asked. He knew his aunt and
his mother would get to the point in their own good
time. But right now, his patience was strained.

"Rosina, you're too long-winded," Florina scolded,
peering at her sister over the rims of her glasses. "You
know Papa always said you were long-winded. You'd
better let me tell him."

Rosina nodded. "You tell him, sister."

"Salvatore," Florina whispered. "This man, he's
been coming around by Annie for the past week, and
we don't like it. He's up to no good. We can just feel
it, right, sister?" Florina touched a hand to her heart.

Rosina looked at her son and nodded solemnly.

Sal felt the hair on the back of his neck prickle. "I
don't understand. Who is this guy? And what does he
have to do with Annie and the deli?" He glanced over
his shoulder at Annie. She'd moved to another aisle
and was busily cleaning up. "Do you think he has
something to do with the burglary?" he asked quietly.

The twins exchanged knowing glances. "That's just
it, Salvatore," his mother offered. "We don't know
what he's up to."

"But we know he's up to no good," Florina inter-
jected firmly. "Right, sister?"

"Right," his mother confirmed, bobbing her head.

Florina leaned close. "Salvatore, you know all those
big developers have been moving into the neighbor-

hood. They've been trying to buy up all the little stores to build skyskuppers."

"Skyskuppers?" Sal repeated blankly.

"Scrapers," his mother corrected, patting her twin's arm. "Skyscrapers, sister. Why, just last week those developers offered Mr. Benedetto ten thousand dollars for his fruit stand." His mother looked shocked, and Sal stiffened. The piece of land the Benedetto fruit stand sat on was worth at least ten times that amount.

"Salvatore." His mother sighed. "What would we do if Mr. Benedetto sold his fruit stand? They have the best tomatoes in the city. Firm but not too sweet. Hardly any acid, either. And it's the only place in the city where we can get good Swiss chard—"

"Not now, sister," Florina scolded, causing Rosina's mouth to click shut. "Not now."

"Anyway," his mother went on. "We're worried. This man is a—"

"Mascalzone Scatsumate," Florina raged, waving her hand in the air. Sal remembered enough Italian to know his aunt wasn't nominating the stranger for sainthood. "Your mama and I, we don't like him and we don't trust him." Florina patted her sister's arm in comfort. "We want you to talk to this man. See what he's up to."

"Yes," his mother agreed, brightening. "Talk to him, Salvatore."

Sal was silent, digesting this information. His cop's instincts suddenly took over. "What does this guy look like?"

"Humph!" Florina exclaimed, nodding her head. "Blond hair and a funny nose."

"What kind of a funny nose?" Sal asked, knowing his aunt had just described about a half a million people in Chicago.

"Small," his mother huffed. "And he smells funny."

"He what?" Sal repeated, mentally trying to translate his mother's and aunt's information.

"And he talks loud," Florina injected, covering her ears with her hands and scowling. "He thinks because we don't speak English so good that we don't hear so good, either. But we hear fine, don't we, sister?" His mother nodded.

Sal mentally tried to form a picture of this strange man that had his mother and aunt so worried. Dancing David's image immediately came to mind. But Sal dismissed it. Why on earth would David want to burglarize the deli? He was obviously affluent. What could he possibly hope to gain? Sal was puzzled. "Ma, do you think you'd recognize this man again, if you saw him?"

She slowly nodded her head. "You know your mama, she never forgets a face."

"I still want Annie to have my bat," Florina insisted, going to retrieve the weapon. Sal gently took it away from her,

"No, Auntie Florina, no weapons. I told you. The police will handle it. I *personally* will find out what's going on."

"You be careful, Salvatore," his mother cautioned, looking worried. Sal smiled, trying to appease her fears.

"Ma, I'm always careful." He leaned down to kiss her cheek.

"And you'll look after Annie?" his aunt asked skeptically. Sal smiled. Looking after Annie had become uppermost in his mind. And until he found out more about Dancing David and the mysterious stranger who had his mother and aunt so worried, he planned to stick close to Annie. Very close. He didn't like the sudden circumstances unfolding around her. But how on earth was he going to convince Annie she needed him around, when all she was trying to do was prove she didn't need him? He'd have to think of something—quick.

"I promise I'll look after Annie."

"And this man, this stranger, you'll see what he's up to?"

"I promise," Sal said solemnly.

"Good," his aunt and mother caroled in unison. "Then let's get to work."

"Tired?" Sal asked, sinking to the now clean floor and pulling Annie close. It had taken nearly four hours to clean up the deli in order for her to open in the morning. There were still some things left to be done: new cold cuts had to be ordered, the front door and the windows had to be replaced, new glass made for the deli case, but at least the interior was presentable enough for the public. Florina and Rosina had finally gone home, and exhausted, Annie wearily sank down on the floor and leaned against Sal.

She knew she should probably keep her distance, considering her growing feelings for him, but she was too tired to do anything but gratefully accept his comfort.

"I'm dead. What a night." Closing her eyes, she burrowed closer to him. Wrapped in the cocoon of Sal's warmth, she forgot her fears. She felt safe and protected, cared for in a way she hadn't felt in a long, long time. She was letting her emotions run away with her, and she knew it. Just because Sal had kissed her once—twice, her mind corrected—was no reason to let her imagination run away with her. She was still the same old Annie to him. The poor widow of his best friend, whom he had to look after.

"Annie?" Sal laid his chin on the top of her head. "I want to talk to you about something."

She stiffened, not liking the sudden seriousness of his tone. They'd successfully avoided talking about what had happened between them all evening. Annie wasn't sure she wanted to talk about it now, not until she'd had a chance to sort out her feelings.

"What?" she asked hesitantly.

"I don't want you to go out with David anymore," he said bluntly. He wasn't ready to tell Annie his suspicions about the man, at least not before he'd done some checking. Annie was frightened enough as it was already, and there was no sense adding to her fears unnecessarily. Until he'd thoroughly checked this guy out, he wasn't about to let him anywhere near Annie.

"I know," Annie said softly, too tired to argue.

"Then you won't see him anymore," Sal said in relief, tightening his arms around her.

She turned her head to look at him, and was caught up short by his nearness. He had the most beautiful eyes, she thought absently. And his mouth—it was soft, warm and inviting, beckoning her closer. She longed to lean forward, to brush her lips across his. Need rippled over her, dulling her senses. No matter how much she longed to kiss Sal, to hold him in her arms just once more, Annie knew she couldn't. She still had some pride left. She wasn't going to be Sal Giordiano's personal burden anymore.

"I didn't say I wouldn't see him again," she said, trying unsuccessfully to avert her gaze. "I said I knew you didn't want me to see him again."

"You mean you're going to go out with him again?" He turned her around to face him, his eyes searching hers.

"Why shouldn't I continue to see David?" she asked, knowing she didn't care if she *ever* saw the man again. "He's very nice, Sal," she protested. "I don't know why you don't like him."

Sal muttered an oath under his breath. "I'm not going to lie to you and say I like David. I don't. I think he's scum."

"Sal!" Annie stared at him. It was so unlike him to lose his temper—at least with her. He had always been calm and easygoing. She was seeing a different side of Sal tonight. Many different sides. "I think you're being unfair to David. He's really a very nice man." She never would have defended David so strongly if Sal hadn't been so obstinate. Never would she admit that David gave her the creeps. If only Sal would understand that she was doing this for his own good.

"'Nice' is hardly the word I'd call him," Sal growled, his eyes darkening. "We had a chat when you went to take those aspirins. It seems that David thinks you've been without..." Sal searched for a delicate way to phrase what he had to say. "David thinks you've been without a man's... *attention* too long, if you know what I mean." He wiggled his brows suggestively and Annie blushed.

She knew what he meant, all right, and it infuriated her to no end to think that the two of them had talked about her lack of..."attention" from a man.

When she was first widowed some of Tony's so-called friends had offered her the same kind of "attention" just to help her through the long, lonely nights. But what Annie missed more than physical closeness was love and affection; the close intimacy that two people who were in love should share. Not even to Sal would she admit that she'd never had that kind of closeness with Tony.

While she'd loved Tony, he'd never really opened up to her. There'd been a part of him she couldn't reach. Their marriage looked ideal from the outside, but inside at times Annie felt very alone and lonely. Even after nearly a year and a half of marriage, she sometimes had a feeling she never really knew her husband. Next time—if there was a next time—she was going to find a man who could share everything with her, be a real, equal partner; someone who would give his all to her, both physically and emotionally. Men like that were hard to find.

She glanced at Sal. He was the kind of man who didn't give his love, physically or emotionally, very often. But she had a feeling that when he did, it would be encompassing and overwhelming. Forever. That's what she was looking for.

Oh, Lord, she *had* to stop thinking about Sal in those terms. Sal wasn't the marrying kind, she reminded herself. And not about to be domesticated, so she'd better not let her imagination run away with her; she would only be looking for trouble.

Her temper flared. "Do you mean to tell me that the two of you were discussing my...my...lack of...?"

"Yes," he said, smiling in spite of himself at the horrified look on her face.

Despite her gratitude for Sal's help and his presence, she wanted to whack him. Again. "My 'attention,'" she said stiffly, trying not to die of mortification, "or lack of it, is hardly what I consider polite dinnertime conversation, for you or David." She shook her head. "I don't believe you two!"

"Oh, you can believe it," Sal assured her with a wicked grin, visibly bracing himself for another outburst. "David seemed to think you were in dire need of—"

"That's enough," she cried in alarm, covering her ears in fear that he would tell her, specifically, what she didn't want to hear.

"Ah, Annie, don't tell me you're mad at me again?" He cocked his head to look at her, his eyes once again going over her features.

She looked into his eyes and felt her stomach drop. Watch yourself, Annie, she cautioned, knowing she was feeling particularly vulnerable now. She didn't know if it was his kiss, or the evening's events, but she was feeling things she shouldn't be feeling.

"Sal, look, I know you don't like the idea of me dating again. But I can't lean on you the rest of my life. Sooner or later you're—" He lifted a hand to stroke her cheek. Wide-eyed, she stared at him, mesmerized by his touch. At the moment, the idea of Annie leaning on him for the rest of her life sounded wonderful.

At the moment she couldn't think of one solid reason why she couldn't lean on him—forever. The thought was comforting, easing some of her fears. Annie mentally shook the thoughts away. She would think of several good reasons as soon as she'd collected her wits, a difficult task with him so near.

"If I'm not complaining," he added, "I don't see why you should be."

No, Sal would never complain. In his mind, what he was doing for her was all wrapped up in his sense of honor and loyalty—admirable qualities, but certainly no reason to take advantage of him. She cared about him too much for that. And until tonight, when he kissed her, she hadn't realized how her feelings for Sal had changed. What she was feeling for him now had nothing to do with friendship, and it frightened her.

"Maybe you're not complaining right now, but what about in the future? Sooner or later one of those buxom blondes is going to catch you. Then what?"

"I don't like buxom blondes," he whispered, gently stroking her cheek.

She wasn't going to tie Sal to her out of some farfetched old-world notion of honor. "I know you feel a certain amount of obligation, but—"

"You think I'm with you now because of some...obligation?" he growled, letting his temper overrule his tongue.

She laughed, the sound thin and harsh. "Of course. Why else? I know you feel a great sense of loyalty to Tony."

"Loyalty has nothing to do with it," he corrected. His gaze dropped to her generous mouth, which was softly parted. As if to prove her a liar, Sal dipped his head, slowly brushing his lips across hers. Annie's eyes widened for a split second before her lashes lowered and she greedily accepted what he offered. Her senses reeled as his mouth fiercely coaxed a response from her.

He knew her so well. She couldn't hide anything from him, not even her deepest feelings or thoughts. He slowly withdrew his lips, his eyes holding hers.

Sal slid his hands to her throat and her eyes closed. He touched the pulse point in her neck, and Annie's breath fled. Her body quivered as he gently caressed her throat. Sal bent and slowly brushed his mouth over hers again, tracing the tender sweetness of her lips with his tongue.

Her pulse went wild at Sal's touch. Sighing with pleasure, she wound her arms around his neck and clung to him as his mouth gently nuzzled her lips. His mouth took hers, possessively, intimately, exploring its honeyed sweetness. There wasn't anything friendly or obligatory about his kiss. It was purely possessive and male, arousing her own feminine instincts in response.

Slowly Sal drew his lips free, resting his forehead against hers, overcome with feelings and emotions. He wanted to keep her safe, and away from anything and anyone that could ever hurt her. "What you need," Sal whispered, hoping he could carry this off, "is a chaperon."

Annie blinked. *Chaperon?* She stared at him in dumb silence. She'd heard the word, she just didn't quite believe it. Sal couldn't be serious.

"A what?" she asked dully, drawing back to look at him in confusion. Sal drew her closer, tucking her into the warmth of his arms.

"A chaperon," Sal repeated helpfully. "You know, someone to look out for your interests. My mother had one, and even Aunt Florina." He grinned at Annie, who looked at him as if he'd just lost his mind. "In our culture it's quite customary."

"Sal, you can't be serious." Her eyes widened as he nodded.

"Of course I'm serious. It's an old family tradition." His eyes twinkled wickedly. "Why, Annie, you're a woman alone with no one to— Ow! Annie, why'd you whack me?" he asked, trying to banish a grin and rub his arm at the same time.

"Sal," she began darkly, flashing him a look that told him exactly what he could do with his "old family tradition." "I'm twenty-six years old, not twelve, and I do *not* need a chaperon!"

"Come on, Annie, it'll be fun—"

"Fun!" Annie exploded. "The whole idea of me dating again was so that I would be less dependent on you, not more! Sal, surely you don't intend to tag after me every time I go out with a man?'' The look on his face answered her question and Annie couldn't suppress a moan. Lord, what was she going to do with him? "This is *not* funny," she told him, pulling out of his arms and getting to her feet.

"It wasn't meant to be," Sal insisted with a wicked grin, dropping an arm around her shoulder and guiding her toward the door.

Sighing in exasperation, Annie flicked off the lights and scooped up her purse. She needed some time to think, to sort through what had happened this evening. And she'd thought she was just going on a simple little date!

Sal took the keys from her and locked up. "First thing in the morning I'll send someone out to fix that door."

"It's not nec—"

Sal held up his hand to override any protests she might have, and urged her down the dark street. "Now don't start with all that *obligation* stuff," he teased, bumping his hip against hers as they rounded the corner and came to her house. She could see the shadow of a smile playing along his full lips.

"You're not really serious about this chaperoning business, are you?"

Sal's smile widened. "Very serious," he assured her, his jaw firmly set.

"Cow cakes," Annie muttered, stomping up the stairs and into the house.

Chapter Five

That man—he's back!" Florina dropped the wheel of cheese she'd been cutting and hurried into the back room, pushing past Annie who was engaged in a heated debate with her insurance agent.

"What man?" Annie asked, eyeing the scurrying woman in alarm.

"That man!" Florina jerked her head toward the front of the store. "The *stranger*," she whispered, her tone of voice loud enough to be heard in her native country. "I'm gonna take care of him." Her eyes gleamed as she waved her bat in the air.

Annie pried the weapon loose from the older woman's hands. "No bats, Florina," she scolded, trying not to smile at the woman's disappointment. "Remember what Sal said. We don't want you hurt. Now go on back out front, I'll be right out." Annie turned her attention back to her insurance man, trying once again to explain that other than the broken glass window, front door and deli case, nothing but fifty dollars in cash and two candy bars were missing. She had a high deductible—almost five hundred dollars—and Annie was certain that the damage to property and goods would be more than that.

After bidding the man a hasty goodbye, Annie grabbed a clean apron and headed to the front of the deli. This morning had been absolute chaos. Word of the robbery had spread throughout the neighborhood. Everyone had been dropping in to check on her, and even Mr. Finucci, all eighty-one years of him, had posted himself outside her broken front door, watching and inspecting anyone who dared enter.

All of her neighbors had closed ranks around her, just as they had when Tony had died. They did their best to make her feel safe and secure. Annie was one of their own, and they intended to see that no further harm came to her.

The outpouring of love and affection had eased her fears somewhat, making her feel less vulnerable. In the light of day, it was hard to imagine that last night she'd been truly frightened. This morning, with the deli open, things looked almost normal. It was as if last night had only been a bad dream.

"Honest," David said nervously, holding his hands in the air. "I assure you I simply want to see how she is." Florina had him backed into a corner. His eyes found Annie's over the top of Florina's head. "Annie, thank God, please come and rescue me from this . . . *woman*."

"Florina!" Annie rounded the corner, shaking her head. So David was the stranger Florina had been so worried about. "It's all right," Annie assured the doubting woman. "This is David Donaldson. He's a friend of mine."

Florina looked at him shrewdly. "'Friend,' humph!" she huffed, giving David one last, scathing look before turning on her heel and heading behind the counter.

"He's back, sister," Florina whispered to Rosina, who was handling the register this morning. "You'd better call Sal. I'll keep an eye on *him*." Nodding, Rosina wiped her hands and slipped into the back room of the deli, which was off-limits to customers. The back room was a combination lunchroom, gossip room and kitchen. This was where Florina and Rosina made their homemade sausage and meatballs for the sandwiches that would be sold to the lunchtime crowd, as well as specialty items like pasta salad, eggplant and other homemade Italian delicacies. The room was small, with a table, a few odd chairs, a television and a telephone squeezed in.

David seized Annie's hands. "My dear, I just heard about the robbery. I'm so sorry, Ann. It must have been awful for you."

Annie smiled at his concern. "It was mostly vandalism, and I'm feeling much better this morning." Out of the corner of her eye, she saw Florina circling around them, inconspicuously trying to duck behind an aisle so she wouldn't be noticed.

"Yes, but still, Ann. I should have stayed with you last night. I—"

"No. Really, David. I'm fine. Sal was here with me, and he helped me clean up." Knowing they had an audience, she gently extracted her hands from his. Annie could see Florina's feet moving up and down the aisles, inching closer and closer.

"Sal," David said, trying not to shudder. "The barbarian. I should have figured."

Annie heard Florina's "Harrumph" at David's words and she bit back a smile. "David, I told you last night, he's not a barbarian. He's a cop."

"Same thing." David draped one long arm around Annie and steered her in the opposite direction, away from the curious stares of the customers and Florina's prying ears. "Didn't I tell you last night that this neighborhood wasn't safe?" David clucked his tongue sympathetically. "I'm telling you, Ann, dear, you're easy prey—"

"David, please." She'd just started feeling better, she didn't need David reminding her of her fears. She was trying so hard not to feel vulnerable, because it only led to her leaning on Sal—something she was determined not to do anymore.

"So tell me," she said with a smile. "What brings you here this morning?" Out of the corner of her eye, Annie saw Florina's gray head pop up from between two aisles.

"I just stopped by to see how you were, and to invite you to supper this evening."

His eyes traveled over her in a way that made her uncomfortable. Crossing her arms across her breasts, Annie was reminded of her conversation with Sal last night, about David's concern about her lack of male "attention." The way he was looking at her, she could almost believe him.

"Things didn't quite work out as I had planned last night," David said smoothly, leaving her to wonder just what his plans had been.

"Yes, I'm sorry about that." How was she going to tell him that she really wasn't interested in dating him? Annie sighed. She never realized this dating business was going to be so darn complicated. And Sal's intentions of chaperoning her weren't going to make things easier in the near future. She certainly didn't want a repeat of last night.

She would have to be gentle with David; she had no wish to hurt his feelings. Even if Sal didn't like him, he was a nice man, but she didn't think she could bear to spend another evening with him, listening to him extol his own virtues. David just didn't appeal to her. She was certain he would be a fine catch for some woman, but not *this* woman. No, the only man she was interested in was tall, dark and devilishly handsome. He also happened to be off-limits.

She'd been telling herself Sal was just a friend. But in the light of day, looking at David, she was forced to come to terms with her own feelings. Last night, when Sal had kissed her, she had finally realized he was much more than just a friend. So much more.

Oh, Lord, Annie thought sadly. The man she wanted she couldn't have. And the one she *could* have, she didn't want. So much for the poor widow woman being able to take care of herself.

"Ann, are you free for dinner?"

"I'm sorry," she said regretfully, shaking her head. "I'd love to, but there's still so much to do here. The glass people are charging me double to come over on a Sunday and I've got to stay here and wait for them. Then I have to try and handle all the insurance forms and the police forms. I just can't spare the time. Maybe another day?" she said brightly, hoping she hadn't hurt his feelings.

David smiled, and patted her shoulder, leaving his hand to linger. "Of course, dear. I understand. Naturally this burglary business has you upset. It's no wonder, with this neighborhood and all, it's a wonder you weren't murdered—or something worse."

Annie shivered at his words.

"Outta my way," Florina grumbled, pushing between the two of them to get to a bin of garlic sitting on the floor. She successfully managed to knock David's hand off Annie's shoulder. David glared at Florina's back.

"That employee is certainly rude. I should think that a woman that age should be grateful for a job."

Clutching the garlic cloves to her breast, Florina straightened and whirled around. "Should have let me use the bat when I had the chance," she muttered in Italian, fixing David with a murderous glare.

"What did she say?" David asked with a frown, watching Florina stomp off.

"She lost her *hat*," Annie said quickly.

"You really ought to speak to her," David suggested. "She's quite insolent. I know this is just a small operation, but you certainly can't have the help scaring the customers away."

"David," Annie cautioned, grabbing him by the elbow and steering him toward the door. It was Rosina's turn to check David out. Her silver head popped up from behind a row of shelves and David came to an abrupt halt, swiveling his head first toward Florina, who stood behind the counter glaring at him, then back to Rosina, who was giving him her own version of the once-over.

"My God! Don't tell me there're *two* of them," he said, horrified. Chuckling softly, Annie rolled her eyes and guided him carefully around the all-too-interested Rosina.

"Those two ladies," she whispered, "are twins. One's Sal's mother and the other is his aunt. They work for me. See, David, while you see this neighborhood as a danger, to me and the other people who have lived here most of our lives, it's really like one big, extended family. Everyone looks after everyone else." She guided him toward the door. She had to get David out of here. The sooner the better. For everyone's sake.

"I should have figured they'd be related to *him*." David pulled open the door and Mr. Finucci appeared out of nowhere. He stood in the doorway, successfully blocking David's path, looking like the angel of death in his dark suit and equally dark fedora, which was pulled low over one eye.

David recognized danger when he saw it and took a cautious step back, keeping his eyes on Mr. Finucci's cane, which swung perilously close to David's unprotected shins.

"What is this, Ann?" David asked, turning to look at her. "A geriatric center?"

Laughing, Annie reached out and patted Mr. Finucci's arm. "It's all right, Mr. Finucci. This is David."

Mr. Finucci nodded, but didn't move.

"Mr. Finucci," she said a bit more loudly, wanting to reassure him. "It's all right. David is a friend of mine."

David extended his hand to the man. Mr. Finucci looked at David's hand, sniffed, then turned, picked up his racing form and reclaimed his perch on the stool next to the door.

"Honestly, Ann, I don't know how you put up with—"

"Oh, Annie!" Mrs. Altero suddenly called from across the street, waving a lace handkerchief and hurrying toward them. "Yoo-hoo!" Mrs. Altero carefully stopped a stream of traffic as she crossed the street. Puffing to a halt, she smiled. "So..." she purred, looking at David with interest. "This is a new friend?"

Word sure traveled fast, Annie thought with amusement. Everyone, no doubt, wanted to get a glimpse of the stranger she'd dated. "Mrs. Altero, I'd like you to meet David Donaldson."

Mrs. Altero batted her lashes. "It's a pleasure to meet you, Donald." She extended her hand, and David just stared at her.

"It's David," he corrected stiffly.

"So... tell me, Donald," Mrs. Altero said, looping her arm through his and steering him toward the street. "Do you like home cooking?"

"Home cooking?" David repeated, glancing over his shoulder at Annie. "Well, yes, I... I love home cooking."

"Wonderful." Mrs. Altero beamed. She knew a pigeon when she saw one. "I've just made a wonderful pot of rabbit stew. You must come and have some."

"But... but... Annie!"

"Don't worry about Annie," Mrs. Altero assured him, dragging him across the street. "She's very busy today. But I'd surely enjoy your company. The table is all set, and we can have a nice chat. It's a shame my granddaughter isn't home. She's a lovely girl."

"Have a nice lunch," Annie called, trying not to laugh at the expression on David's face. She had to admit that she felt a little guilty at letting him be bamboozled by Mrs. Altero. Anyway, maybe if he got to know some of the people in the neighborhood, he would realize how very special Little Italy was, and why she would never move.

Annie turned and started to head back into the deli. A dark blue sedan screeched around the corner, coming to a halt in front of her. Annie shaded her eyes from the harsh afternoon sun and watched as Sal jumped from the car.

Her pulse danced a merry pace at the sight of him. God, he looked wonderful. He had on soft, faded jeans that were nearly worn through in spots and fit his muscular legs like a second skin. A white polo shirt with the collar open and turned up, stretched wide across his broad shoulders. Tennis shoes—carelessly untied—covered his feet. He looked like a man who was going somewhere in a hurry.

He glanced around as if he were looking for someone before bringing his gaze to hers. He smiled, and her heart began to thud wickedly. "Hi," he said simply, shoving his keys into the pocket of his jeans and coming around the car toward her. "How is everything today?"

"Everything is just fine." Annie rocked back on her heels and returned his smile. "What brings you here this time of the afternoon?" Whatever the reason, Annie was glad to see him. His presence made her feel vulnerable, yet cared for. He couldn't hide the concern in his dark eyes. So much had changed in just the past few days, Annie thought. So much. Their relationship. Her feelings. Oh, Lord. She had to stop this, she was driving herself crazy. She was supposed to be learning to stand on her own feet, not depending on him more and more.

"Just came to see how you were." He smiled into her eyes, lifting a hand to brush a strand of hair off her cheek. Her skin burned from his touch, coming alive from the warmth of him. All of her sincere efforts to keep her feelings about Sal in perspective crumbled the moment he came near. "After all, what are chaperons for?" he asked with a grin.

"Sal," she began, wanting to put an end to this nonsense before it got out of hand. "I really wish—"

"Come on, let's go inside, I'm starving." Sal dropped his hand to her back and guided her into the store, pausing to wink at Mr. Finucci, who gave him a thumbs-up signal in return. He'd told his mother to pass the word: if David showed up, they were supposed to call him—and then keep David occupied until he could get there. Evidently they'd done a fine job. Annie was safe, and Dancing David was nowhere in sight.

It was just too much of a coincidence for his cop's intuition that last night, the first night Annie had been gone for the evening, the deli had been robbed. He didn't have any concrete evidence, nothing to back his suspicions on, but he had a gut feeling Dancing David was somehow connected to the burglary. How, he didn't know yet, but he'd already done some checking this morning. Until he found out just what the hell was going on he didn't want David anywhere near Annie—at least not without him around.

Annie looked at Sal carefully. "David was just here," she announced unnecessarily. She had a feeling she was telling him something he already knew.

"Don't forget you owe me a game," Mr. Finucci growled as they passed. He leaned forward to try to pinch Annie, but she stepped out of his reach just in the nick of time.

"What was all that about?" Annie wanted to know.

"All what, Annie?" Sal repeated vaguely, trying unsuccessfully to banish a grin.

"The wink and the grin, and the 'You owe me a game' stuff. What are you up to, Sal?"

"Me?" He drew back looking greatly offended. "What makes you think I'm up to something? I just promised Mr. Finucci a game of boccie, that's all." Sal paused, bending over the counter to plant a kiss on his mother's and his aunt's cheeks. They, too, flashed him a thumbs-up signal and Annie sighed.

Something was definitely going on here. But she had a feeling neither Sal, his mother, his aunt, Mrs. Altero *nor* Mr. Finucci, for that matter, were going to let her in on it.

"Aunt Florina, cut me a piece of that cheese, will you?" Sal plucked the cheese from his aunt's hand and rounded the corner to the cooler with Annie on his heels. Retrieving a cold soda, he took a long sip, knowing Annie was watching him.

"I didn't have lunch," he explained, leaning against the wall.

"Do you want a sandwich? I can fix you one."

Sal shook his head and finished off his cheese. "So, tell me, how is David?" The man's name was beginning to get on his nerves. He didn't like him, and it wasn't just because he was interested in Annie, although that was part of it—a large part.

Sal cocked his head and studied Annie. Something was happening to him, something he didn't understand. Ever since he'd kissed her, he'd had an uneasy feeling in his gut. And he didn't like it one bit.

He had his life-style down pat—no commitments, no strings. He'd been happy, or so he'd thought, until a few days ago. Now he wasn't so sure. Holding Annie in his arms, he realized something had been missing from his life. Love.

Ever since he'd kissed her he couldn't get her out of his mind. Last night he had lain awake all night, wondering what it would be like to have her with him. His thoughts scared the hell out of him, yet filled him with a strange and wonderful buoyancy. She was no longer just the widow of his best friend, but a beautiful, desirable woman.

Smooth, Suave Sal. He smiled to himself. That wasn't him, not really; it was an image, not the man inside. The man inside was scared as hell right now because what he was feeling for Annie was unlike anything he'd ever felt before.

Her smile, her laugh, the way her eyes lit with pleasure, everything about her was so familiar and yet so achingly new. He wanted more than just a few kisses, more than a few caresses; he wanted Annie, and he didn't know what the hell to do about it.

"David is fine," Annie said glumly, wondering what was going on behind Sal's dark eyes.

"What did he want?"

"He wanted me to have supper with him tonight."

"And?" One dark brow rose in question.

"And that's it," she answered, knowing her evasiveness would annoy him. It did.

"So are you?" he asked, after thoughtfully chewing his cheese.

Annie sighed. "Am I what, Sal?"

"Having supper with Dancing David?" Sal's eyes tracked her, watching as she nervously pinched a piece of her apron between two fingers.

"No." She shook her head, and he heaved a sigh of relief. "I've got too much to do here today," she lied, not wanting Sal to know she had no intention of dating David again. "I have to wait for the glass repairman, and fill out insurance forms and—"

"Did you discover anything else missing?" Sal asked casually. Two candy bars were hardly worth breaking in for. He had a feeling the burglary was something more than it seemed, but he hadn't yet figured out what it was.

"Sal, do you know something?" Annie asked suspiciously. "Something that you're not telling me?"

"I don't know." Sal shrugged his shoulders and grinned. "There're probably a lot of things I know that I haven't got around to telling you. Anything specific you had in mind?" Until he had some concrete proof of his suspicions, he didn't want to tell Annie anything. There was no point in alarming her any further. He was certain she was safe, but just in case, Sal intended to stick close to her—very close—just to make sure she was. He wasn't about to let anyone or anything harm her. He'd waited too long for her.

"The burglary, Sal? Do you know something about it you're not telling me?" A chill of fear washed over her again, and she shivered.

"No, nothing definite," he assured her, shaking his head and wanting to change the subject. "So, tell me, how did David find out about the burglary?"

"I don't know," she answered truthfully, frowning. "Someone from the neighborhood must have told him."

Sal doubted it. He added it to the list of things to check out. David was a stranger, and strangers weren't easily welcomed or trusted. David was no exception. He stuck out like a pair of brown shoes with a tuxedo.

"He was quite concerned," she added, wanting to prove to Sal that David was harmless. "It's funny, because just last night, before you joined us, David was trying to talk me into moving out of the neighborhood because he doesn't think it's safe."

Sal straightened abruptly as warning bells began to clang ominously in his head. "He what?" Sal grabbed Annie's elbow and dragged her into the back room so they wouldn't be overheard.

"Sal," she cried, trying to get free. "What on earth are you doing? What has gotten into you?" Annie yanked her arm free, staring up at him in astonishment. "What on earth has come over you the past few days?"

"Annie," he said gravely, dropping his hands to her shoulders. "I want you to tell me exactly what David said last night. Do you hear me? Everything. And don't leave anything out."

"Everything?" she repeated in alarm. "How can I possibly remember everything we talked about? And what difference does it make? Sal, if you're going to start acting like a deranged father ag—"

"Annie, please." Sighing, Sal dragged a hand through his hair. He needed this information, but he didn't want to alarm her. "Could you please just indulge me?"

"But why?" She'd never seen Sal so intense, so serious. This wasn't just some macho inquisition, this was something else altogether.

"Annie, please?"

Sal never asked her for anything. If he wanted a blow-by-blow account of her boring conversation with

David, she would give it to him. "Last night," she began carefully, "David was giving me a lecture about his stocks, his bonds, his Remingtons—"

"His what?" Sal frowned.

"Remingtons," she repeated with a heavy sigh. "They're paintings. When he took me to his apartment, I was admiring his—"

Sal's jaw tightened. "He took you to his apartment!"

"No," she snapped, growing annoyed at his interrogation. "He changed his clothes in the back seat of the car! Of course he took me to his apartment. And stop scowling like that, Sal."

"All right, all right. Go on. Then what?"

"We drove to the restaurant, and we talked about—" She stopped, not wanting to tell Sal that they'd talked about *him*. She had a feeling David's rather caustic comments about Sal wouldn't further endear David to him. "We talked about the neighborhood," she hedged. "He said he was concerned about my welfare. You know, the poor widow woman living alone." She tried to make light of it, but apparently Sal's sense of humor was out of joint this morning.

"Is that all?"

"Well," she fumed, "I'm sure there would have been more if we hadn't been so rudely interrupted!"

He grinned. "Are you implying that I was rude?"

Annie glared at him. "What would you call muscling in on my date, and getting us thrown out of a restaurant?"

"A smart move," he quipped, his grin widening. He glanced at his watch. He was waiting for a call that would answer some questions about Dancing David.

"Sal, why all this interest in David and our date? I know you don't like him, but—"

"Do you?" he asked abruptly. His eyes held hers until her knees felt weak. "Do you like him, Annie?" he asked again, tipping her chin up until her gaze met his. Annie took a deep breath as his clean male scent washed over her.

Utterly disgusted at the sudden flare of hope in her heart, Annie made a heroic effort to control her feelings. Sal was just asking because *he* didn't like David and he was concerned for her welfare. Not for any other reason, she assured herself. And she'd better not start thinking any differently.

But last night after she'd crawled into bed, she hadn't been able to stop thinking about Sal, or his kisses. She kept reliving it over and over in her mind. She realized that Sal was everything a woman could ever want—patient, kind, loving, giving. But just because the man had kissed her was no reason for her to start entertaining thoughts she had no business entertaining.

They'd been through so much together the past two years, it was only natural that he felt an emotional attachment to her, and she for him.

But that was all it was, nothing more. It was common for people who'd gone through something tragic together to form an emotional attachment. Grief had a way of binding people together, but, she reminded herself, she couldn't read anything more into it.

Sal ran his thumb over her chin, gently touching the racing pulse point in her throat. Annie swallowed hard. All her defenses seemed to crumble when he was near.

"Do you?" he repeated, gently teasing the tender skin of her throat, and Annie's mind shifted into panic.

"He's...nice," she hedged, trying to ignore the fact that Sal had slipped his arms around her waist.

"Are you going out with him again?" he asked, drawing her close. Despite her resolutions to keep her feelings about Sal in perspective, Annie laid her head on his shoulder, sighed, then gave in to the sensations of the moment. It certainly would help matters if she didn't feel so right in Sal's arms. It was nothing, she assured herself. Her emotions were only natural, considering the circumstances. But at the moment, locked in Sal's arms, she was having a hard time keeping things objective.

"Sal...would you like to come over for dinner tonight?"

He tensed. "I'd love to, Annie, but I can't. I've...I've got a date."

Annie stiffened and stepped out of his arms. "I see," she said, trying not to show her intense annoyance. *She* couldn't go out without a chaperon, but it was all right for him to continue his carousing! She wasn't jealous, she told herself. Why should she be jealous? Sal had gone on hundreds of dates over the past few years, so why should this one be any different?

"Annie." Sal grabbed her arm, knowing she misunderstood. "I promised Mrs. Altero I'd come over for dinner—"

"And meet her granddaughter?"

Sal nodded. He had to talk to Mrs. Altero. She was the only one who'd been around last night and she was the only clue he had. She'd even taken a walk past the deli just about the time of the burglary. If it meant eating her cooking and meeting her granddaughter in an effort to obtain the information he needed to protect Annie, then he would do it. He would worry about explaining to Annie later. Right now, he just wanted to make sure she was safe.

"Yes," he sighed, "and meet her granddaughter. I shouldn't be late, though, and I'll be right across the street if you need me."

"Need you," she fumed. "Sal, come on, I told you, I'm a big girl and it's about time I start handling my own life and my own affairs. Now, I've got to get back to work." She shrugged off his arm and headed out front.

"Annie?"

She stopped, holding her breath. "What, Sal?"

"You never answered my question. Are you going out with David again?"

Annie turned to him with a grin. "You're right, I never *did* answer your question, did I? Have a good time tonight," she called, giving his cheek a friendly pat before turning and heading back to her waiting customers.

Chapter Six

Annie paced the length of the living room, not knowing what to do with herself. She kept going from window to window, peering at Mrs. Altero's house, wondering what Sal was doing, and knowing he was there—with the infamous granddaughter.

She'd already drunk four cups of herbal tea, finished filling out all the forms that needed filling out, washed all her floors, and still she kept pacing. Lord, this wasn't supposed to be happening. Sal was supposed to be worried about the men *she* was dating—not the other way around.

Sighing at her own behavior, Annie went into the kitchen and poured herself another cup of tea. She wasn't thirsty, she just needed to do *something* to keep her mind off Sal.

She didn't want to think about him. But she couldn't seem to stop herself. The more she thought about Sal, the more confused she felt.

Sipping her tea, she went back into the living room and sank down in the rocker. What was she going to do? She had to think about this problem rationally, she realized, glancing around the familiar room.

She'd spent hours refurbishing the old brownstone after Tony had died. They had bought the house right after they'd gotten married because it was close to the police station and the deli. She'd grown up in an almost identical house not two blocks away.

After Tony's death, with nothing but grief and time on her hands, she'd stripped all the woodwork, refinishing it to its original beauty. Sal had helped her do some of the heavy work, spending his days off and vacation time hauling wood, scraping off paint and just lending a hand wherever needed. They'd discovered they both had a fondness for country furnishings and flea-market finds, so they'd spent many a Sunday getting up at dawn hunting down bargains.

Everywhere she looked now, she saw the touch of Sal's hand. The pineapple stencil he'd carefully painted around the perimeter of the floors; the blue print wallpaper he'd helped her hang; the old chandelier—one of their flea-market finds—that he'd purchased for a song and then carefully rewired and hung. The house and deli had been her comfort, something to hang on to, something safe and secure after Tony's death. It gave her a way of easing the lonely hours. With Sal around, her loneliness didn't seem so acute, so hard to bear.

But for some reason, tonight, the loneliness was back, and worse than ever.

Sal. He invaded her thoughts again. They'd had such a wonderful relationship—a friendly relationship—until she'd announced she had a date. Sal had changed from a warm, caring, concerned friend into a man who seemed obsessed with protecting her virtue.

Then he had to go and kiss her, she thought with a frown. And not just a friendly peck on the cheek, but a man-woman kiss, the kind that shook her to her soul. Annie's lashes lowered and a great fountain of warmth washed over her as she relived the touch of Sal's lips on hers.

That certainly wasn't a friendly kiss; it was a kiss filled with yearning. So what was he doing with Mrs. Altero's granddaughter? Trying to drive her crazy, probably, she decided.

Annie rocked faster, feeling restless. Sal was a man who was used to this type of thing. Kissing one woman one day, and dating another the next. He'd dated women galore and had lots of experience.

But she hadn't. Despite the fact that she was twenty-six, married and widowed in the space of two years, her knowledge and experience with men was nil. She'd never really even kissed anyone except Tony. And now that seemed so very long ago she could hardly remember. At times she couldn't even picture Tony's face.

She'd come to her marriage a virgin, and since Tony's death there had been no one else. She'd never even *wanted* anyone else. Until now.

Setting her cup on a table, Annie stopped rocking and abruptly stood up to go to the window again, letting the air cool her flushed face. She wasn't falling in love with Sal, she told herself firmly. What she was feeling was an emotional attachment. She was just having a hard time separating the two.

A faint breeze rustled the curtains, filling the room with the night's sweet aroma. The pungent smell of sausage and peppers drifted through the open window, the remnants of someone's dinner, no doubt.

The street was quiet tonight. In the summer, it wasn't unusual to find lawn chairs scattered up and down the block, with neighbors gathered to gossip or watch a baseball game on a television that someone had dragged out. The kids would run free, playing baseball or tag. Invariably someone would bring out a pitcher of lemonade or a jug of wine, and they would sit discussing the day's events or just listening to music long into the night. Tonight the street was empty except for an occasional car. Even Mr. Benedetto hadn't taken his nightly walk.

It was strange to see the street so quiet. Annie sighed. Perhaps the burglary had had more of an effect than she realized. Shivering, Annie wrapped her arms around herself.

"Hey, Annie, waiting for someone?" Sal stood beneath the window with a wide grin on his face. Her startled gaze flew to his. Oh, Lord, he knew she'd been watching—waiting for him. Her heart began to pound and her face flooded with heat. Now she'd done it, really made a fool of herself, standing here pacing

back and forth from window to window, watching and
wondering what he was doing.

And he'd caught her.

She glanced down at him, gathering her dignity.
He'd dressed for his dinner with Mrs. Altero and her
granddaughter, she noted, taking in the gray pinstripe
suit. His jacket was slung over his shoulder and his silk
print tie was at half-mast. The sleeves of his light blue
shirt were rolled up, revealing muscular forearms. He
looked, in a word, wonderful.

"I wasn't waiting for anyone," she replied coolly,
determined not to let him know she'd been waiting for
him. From the look on his face, she had a feeling he
knew.

"You sure?" He grinned, and she stiffened indig-
nantly, aggravated that he was so arrogant as to guess
exactly what she'd been doing.

"Positive," she snapped succinctly. "I was just
getting a breath of fresh air."

"Are you busy?" He didn't give her a chance to
answer. "Come on out. We can sit on the porch for a
while."

"It's . . . it's . . . late," she stammered, not knowing
if she trusted herself to be alone with him. It was
odd—all this time, she'd never given it a second
thought. They'd been alone many, many times in the
past, then; but she'd never been so aware of Sal as a
man before.

Sal generally stopped by after his dates. Usually she
was sitting out front with the neighbors, and he would
tell her all about his evening, where he went, with
whom. But that was before she needed to keep a safe

distance from him—at least until she was certain she could separate her emotions and keep things in perspective.

And she wasn't entirely certain she *wanted* to sit and listen to Sal discuss what a wonderful evening he'd had with another woman, any more than he'd enjoyed her going into detail about her evening with David!

"It's not that late, Annie. Come on, you can get a breath of fresh air out here. Besides, I'm lonely."

"Lonely," she snapped. "Why didn't you stay with Mrs. Altero's granddaughter? I'm sure she would have been more than happy to ease your . . . loneliness."

"Are you jealous, Annie?" he asked, his lips curling up in a bemused smile that only aggravated her more.

"Jealous!" she fumed. "Don't be ridiculous. I'll have you know, Detective Giordiano, I don't have a jealous bone in my body."

"I brought you a present," he said, trying to entice her. She looked down at him in surprise. The streetlight cast a golden glow on his hair, making it appear even blacker.

"What kind of a present?" she asked suspiciously.

"Tell you what. You come down and check out your present." He grinned suddenly. "And I'll check out your bones—just to make sure you don't have any jealous ones," he assured her, his grin sliding wider.

The man was impossible. Charming but impossible, and she had absolutely no intention of going outside to see him.

"I'll be right down," she called. Turning from the window, Annie grabbed a sweater and went out, letting the screen door slam behind her.

Sal was sitting on the porch, leaning against the railing with his long legs stretched out in front of him. He looked up at her and smiled. "Pull up a step." He patted the space right next to him, and against her better judgment she sat down.

"So, where's my present?" she finally asked, forcing her voice to remain neutral.

Sal turned to look at her. His eyes were twinkling with mischief. He dug into his suit jacket, which was folded neatly on the stairs. Frowning, Annie stared blankly at the hard white mass he dropped into her hand.

She frowned. "What is this? A baseball?"

Sal laughed. "It's a dumpling. Or at least that's what Mrs. Altero claimed it was. You should have seen me trying to smuggle it out of there."

She laughed softly. "What on earth did you have for dinner?"

He groaned and rubbed his stomach. "Indigestion."

Annie laughed. "Poor thing." Served him right, she thought smugly. "It's your own fault," she scolded. "You could have had dinner with me." The moment the words were out, she was sorry. He tilted his head to look at her, a curious expression in his eyes.

"I would have much preferred to have dinner with you, Annie," he said quietly, looking directly into her eyes until she glanced away. Oh, Lord, he was back to the industrial-strength charm again, she thought in alarm.

Sal reached out and laced his fingers through hers. "So, what did you do tonight?"

Annie shifted uncomfortably. She'd never felt awkward or uncomfortable talking to Sal before. But now, sitting so near to him, having her hand encased in his, she felt an air of electricity between them. It was as thick as syrup and just as hard to ignore. She was just so aware of him beside her, looking at her, smiling at her.

"Paperwork, housework." She shrugged. *Thought about you.*

He tightened his fingers on her hand and tugged her closer. "Why are you sitting so far away? I won't bite." His thigh brushed against hers and she trembled.

"How's Dancing David?" he inquired, trying to sound casual.

"I don't know, I haven't seen him since he came into the store this morning."

"Good." He turned his head away from her to glance down the street.

"You really don't like him, do you Sal?"

He turned to face her. "Do you?" he asked again. His eyes held hers. Great waves of warmth rippled over her as they stared at each other in the darkness of the night.

"He's...he's..." Annie licked her lips as Sal gently caressed her hand.

"I know, he's clean and nice," he said, parroting her own words. "Come here, Annie," he whispered, and she went, scooting closer to him until they were sitting thigh to thigh. He wrapped his arm around her waist and drew her close, turning her around until she was cradled with her back against the soft pad of his chest. Sighing, Annie tried to relax, tried to calm the frantic pounding of her heart. She laid her head back and closed her eyes as Sal wrapped his arms around her.

She inhaled deeply. His heady fragrance of musk and maleness teased and delighted her senses.

"I'm just checking your bones," he whispered in her ear, running his hands slowly up and down her arms in a leisurely caress. "Annie?"

She shivered. "What, Sal?"

"Can I ask you something?"

"What?"

"Would you go out with me?"

She smiled in the darkness. "Sal, I *am* out with you."

"No, Annie," he said quietly. "I mean really out with me. On a date." He'd wrestled with the idea all day long, trying to come to grips with his feelings for Annie and his guilt. His feelings had won out, finally.

"A date?" Annie swallowed hard as her heart gave a great leap.

A crooked grin tilted the corners of his mouth. "Yeah, you know, like the one you went on with Dancing David. Me, you, dinner, maybe some dancing or a show. What do you say?"

Momentarily stunned, Annie sat perfectly still. The only sound in the night's darkness was their mingled breaths and her pounding heart.

"Sal," she began carefully. "Don't you think you're carrying this chaperoning thing a bit far?"

He grabbed her shoulders, shifting her so she was half lying across his lap, her face hovering just below his. His eyes went over her face and he felt a sudden tightening in his loins. At the moment, chaperoning was the last thing on his mind.

"What does going on a date with me have to do with chaperoning?" he asked quietly, and Annie sighed, trying hard not to look into his beautiful eyes.

"Sal, why are you asking *me* for a date all of a sudden?"

"Well," he said, lifting a finger to tease a tendril of hair that had slipped across her cheek. "You're nice and clean—" He stopped. "I do believe you told me those were the qualities one should appreciate in a date," he explained, and Annie laughed.

"I know," she murmured, feeling confused. "But why—"

"Annie," he said quietly, his eyes searching hers. "I care about you."

He was so close she could see the laugh lines around his mouth, see the tenderness in his eyes. It made her heart ache with longing. Annie reached up and touched his face. He needed a shave and she loved the gritty texture of his face. "And I care about you."

Sal frowned in confusion, clearly not understanding. "Then what's the problem?"

"Sal, do you remember right after Tony died?" She waited for his nod, trying to ease the confusion in his eyes. "I was so lost, so alone. And then you came to my rescue like a knight in shining armor," she said softly, reaching up to touch his face again. He caught her hand and held it. "You always knew just the right thing to do, the right thing to say. You always made me feel so much better about myself, about everything." Her eyes sought his for understanding. "Whenever I needed you, no matter what the reason, I knew I could count on you. I never felt quite so alone when you were around." She smiled tenderly. "I'll always be grateful to you, Sal—"

"Annie," he growled. "You have nothing to be grateful for."

"Please, let me finish. It's only natural for us to feel an emotional bond to one another. We've been through so much together. Sharing the pain of Tony's death, of course it would draw us together. Grief has a way of doing that," she said sadly, pausing to take a deep breath. "But you don't have to worry about me anymore, Sal. I know you felt like you owed it to Tony to look after me, but I can't be your personal burden any longer."

"Annie." The tone of his voice caused her to glance up at him. Her eyes went over his face, and her heart constricted. He was so handsome. He made her feel things she'd never felt before, things that touched the walls of her soul.

"If you think," he said quietly, "that I want to go out with you because I'm emotionally attached to you because of some strange idea you have about us being bound together, you're wrong."

"Sal, what you're feeling is perfectly normal under the circumstances. You feel protective and possessive, but it doesn't mean anything. It will pass."

"Annie," he growled, slipping a finger under her chin and lifting her face so she was forced to look in his eyes. "What I'm feeling is not going to pass; this isn't the mumps, you know." What he was feeling had a name, but he was almost afraid to think it, let alone say it. He had to come to terms with his own guilt first.

Annie glanced away, wondering exactly what it was he was feeling. Protectiveness, certainly. Possessiveness, definitely, but anything beyond that she was certain was only a reflex action. If only he would listen to her and believe her. She had to keep them both from getting carried away.

"Sal, I think—" His mouth covered hers and a whimper of pleasure escaped her when Sal's lips touched hers. Annie arched against him, tightening her arms and drawing him close. She sighed in contentment as Sal's tongue parted her lips and his kiss deepened.

He gently caressed the length of her back, his touch warm against the thin cotton of her shirt, heating her skin. His arms cradled her as her senses reeled. Annie moved her hands restlessly, gently roaming across his broad shoulders and back.

His tongue teased her, coaxing a willing response until a yearning ignited deep inside. She clung to him, whimpering softly, following his lead, doing as he did and enjoying the wild sensations he aroused in her.

"Sal, please," she whispered, gently pushing him away. "We have to stop."

He lifted his head, his eyes glittering with desire. "Why, Annie?"

She inched out of his arms. It would be easier to talk—to think—if he wasn't so close. "Because," she said softly, struggling to regain some composure. This wasn't going to help the situation between them. One of them had to keep their head. "Sal, I know you're used to this kind of thing."

"What the hell does that mean?" he growled. "What do you mean, 'this kind of thing'?"

She took a deep breath. "You have a lot of experience with... I...I...don't want to be just another one of your... women."

Sal swore under his breath. "Annie, you would never be just another woman. Don't you know that? What's happening between us—"

She stopped the flow of his words with her fingertips. "What's happening between us is perfectly normal," she said, knowing the words were a lie. What was happening to her was warm and wonderful, and not in the least normal.

"Annie, listen." He tried to put his arms around her again, but she held him at bay. "You really think this is some kind of attachment thing?"

"Yes," she said with a conviction she no longer felt.

"And what if it's not, Annie? What if it's something more?" His eyes met hers and her heart did a nosedive. "Are you willing to dismiss it so easily?"

Oh, Lord. Annie turned away, tearing her gaze from his to stare down the darkened street. What he was saying was everything she'd been feeling but had tried to deny.

"Annie," he said quietly. "I know I've had a lot of... experience with women. Maybe that's why I'm so sure this isn't an attachment thing, or something that will pass, but something more."

His words caused a lump to form in her throat and Annie turned to look at him. His eyes looked bleak and forlorn. She reached out and covered his hand with hers.

"I've never felt this way before," Sal admitted, a sad smile on his face. "And I feel guilty as hell, too. I probably shouldn't be feeling what I do, Annie. God! You're my best friend's wife—"

"Widow," she corrected softly. "I'm a widow, Sal."

"Yeah, widow," he said with a wry grimace. "All I know is that if you have any doubt at all about this attachment thing, then all I want is a chance, Annie. A chance," he repeated. "And then one way or another we'll know for sure. So what do you say? Will you go out with me?" Something flickered in his eyes, and she smiled as her heart filled with joy.

"Yes," she whispered. "I'll go out with you."

He grinned, grabbing her up and hugging her tightly. "There's just one thing, Annie."

She could feel his heart thudding through the thin fabric of his shirt. It matched the wicked rate of her own. "What, Sal?"

"I'm not wearing a damn skirt," he grumbled.

Annie laughed softly. "Good. I prefer my men to wear pants."

Her men. Sal tightened his arms around her. If he had his way, there would be no other men in Annie's life. Ever. Now, all he had to do was convince her of that.

Chapter Seven

"Annie! Don't you look lovely." Rosina looked up from the shelves she'd been stocking and frowned. "Going out with Salvatore again?" Rosina asked hopefully, a wide smile on her wrinkled face.

"Yes," Annie confirmed. For the past few weeks she'd spent nearly every evening with Sal. They'd gone to a couple of baseball games, out to dinner, to the show. Their relationship had progressed to another level, and now Annie knew for certain there was more than just friendship between them. She could no longer deny the fact that she was falling in love with Sal.

"Do I look all right?" she asked, fingering the collar of the white silk sheath dress she wore. She'd caught her new curls up atop her head, fastening them with a pair of white pearl combs. Pearl earrings and white high-heeled sandals completed her outfit.

"You look lovely," the older woman insisted, touching Annie's face gently. "Just lovely. You know, Annie, it's time," Rosina said softly, her eyes glowing warmly.

"Time?" Annie frowned. "Time for what?"

"Time for you to find another man." She held up her hand as Annie started to protest. "I know—I know—it's none of my business. But I love you like my own, Annie, and it's not good for you to be alone. You need a man in your life." Rosina smiled. "Someone like my Salvatore."

"Rosina," Annie said carefully, not wanting his mother to get her hopes up. "Sal and I are just—friends." She was beginning to hate the sound of that word. "Sal just cares for me because he feels loyal to Tony."

"No, Ann Marie." Rosina shook her head, her eyes twinkling. "I'm not blind. I see the way he looks at you. The way you look at him. It's time for Salvatore, too. Time for him to settle down."

"Rosina, you don't understand. Sal's not the kind of man to settle down." She tried to smile. "The only woman he plans to have a serious relationship with is Sara Lee. He's as slippery as greased lightning and just as quick. He told me so."

Rosina frowned, confused. "What is this—greasy lightning? And who is this Sara? I don't know this woman."

Annie laughed softly. She'd forgotten Rosina didn't understand slang. And there was no way to literally translate any of it into Italian. She searched for words to try to explain. "It means Sal's not about to settle down with one woman. He wants them all. And Sara is ... Never mind," Annie said with a laugh. Florina, who baked everything from scratch, would be appalled to learn her son had a passion for store-bought frozen bakery goods.

"No, no." Rosina shook her head. "Salvatore—he sees lots of women because he just hasn't found the right one. Giordiano men take their time to find the right woman—but when they do..." Rosina smiled dreamily, patting Annie's cheek. "Papa and mama were married almost fifty years. And Salvatore's father and I, we were married almost as long." She sighed heavily, clutching a hand to her breast. "When a Giordiano man finds the right woman—ahh! She will be a lucky woman, Annie. Salvatore, he will make a good husband. Very good."

Annie knew without a doubt Sal would make a good husband. If he ever settled down. *Sal's woman.* Just the thought brought a tingle of pleasure. What would it be like to belong to him and have his love in return? Heaven, she realized.

But, she acknowledged sadly, that didn't change the fact that just because his mother wanted things to work out, they would. Rosina didn't understand. But *she* did, all too well. And Annie knew there was no point in trying to explain it. She'd told Sal she would give it a try, but she also knew a leopard couldn't change its spots. Sal wasn't the kind of man to be domesticated—right woman or not.

Annie glanced at the large overhead clock. "Rosina, I'm going to go outside to wait for Sal. He said he would be here about six."

Rosina nodded. "You go and have a good time. Florina and I will close up. Have fun. Just remember what I said."

Nodding, Annie went outside, closing the door softly behind her. It was still warm out, but the sky was gray, threatening rain. She stood for a moment, trying to decide if she needed her raincoat. The air smelled heavy and damp.

David's car slid to a halt in front of her. Over the past few weeks he'd stopped by occasionally, but almost as soon as David showed up, Sal seemed to appear out of nowhere. It was odd, almost as if Sal had a radar device on David.

"Ann," David called, rolling down the window. "Hi. Get in."

"Just for a moment," she said, opening the door and climbing in. "I'm waiting for Sal." Since the night she'd told David she couldn't have supper with him, he'd repeatedly asked her out, but she had steadfastly refused. There was no point in leading the man on. He was pleasant enough, but her heart belonged to someone else, and it would have been cruel to give David false hope. Yet, despite her gentle rebuffs David still kept coming around, much to Sal's chagrin.

"You look lovely, Ann," David said, letting his eyes rest on the gentle curve of her breast. The way he looked at her made her feel extremely uncomfortable. She remembered what Sal had said about David's concern about her lack of male "attention", and she flushed.

"Thank you," she interrupted, shifting uncomfortably.

"You like Sal, don't you?" David's lips thinned in displeasure.

Annie smiled. "Yes, very much."

David's lips thinned. "I figured as much. I never thought I'd get beat out by—well, never mind." He reached out and slowly stroked her bare arm, sending a clammy sense of apprehension rippling over her. "It's a shame, Ann. Really. I'd thought—" He smiled grimly. "Well, it doesn't matter now."

"I'm sorry," Ann whispered, wishing she'd never even gotten into the car with him. She was beginning to feel very, very nervous. What ever made her think David was pleasant and harmless? The expression on his face was neither pleasant nor harmless. "David, you're very nice and sweet, but I'm not ... I'd like us to just be friends. I hope you understand."

David nodded, but he didn't look particularly understanding. "Tell me, Ann, what do you see in that—"

"Yoo-hoo, David!" Mrs. Altero leaned out her window and waved. Annie heaved a sigh of relief.

"Oh, no," he groaned, slouching lower in his seat. "Ann, that woman is a menace! She should be locked up somewhere. She fed me this awful-looking mess that smelled like dirty socks, and—"

"David," Annie began slowly, trying not to laugh. "Mrs. Altero is a wonderful woman, just naturally friendly. I'm sure she was just trying to be kind."

"Kind!" He snorted in disgust. "This neighborhood is filled with kooks. I don't know why you insist on staying here. It's not only not safe, but detrimental to a human being's intellectual growth. Half the people here can't even speak the language. And the smells—'' David shuddered. ''I'm telling you, Ann, you're taking your life in your hands if you insist on staying. First a burglary, and then who knows what. I wish you would reconsider. I'm sure I could get you a good price for the deli, and the house. I don't see why you won't—''

''David, please.'' She held up her hands, not wanting another lecture. ''I told you before, I'm not going anywhere. Not ever.''

''There's a nice apartment open in my building. I'm sure if I talk to the leasing agent—''

''David, I've got to go.'' Prepared to bolt, she grabbed the door handle, but David laid a hand on her arm, his fingers digging into the soft, bare flesh.

''David!'' Annie cried, shocked. ''You're hurting me.''

''I'm sorry,'' David said, loosening his grip but not releasing her. ''But I wish you'd reconsider, or at least think about it. If you change your mind about—''

She yanked her arm free. ''I'm not going to change my mind, David, but thank you for offering.'' Annie threw open the door and jumped out. Absently rubbing her arm, she heaved a sigh of relief when she saw his little import tear away from the curb.

David was a very strange man; and seemingly obsessed with safety. If he only knew that in the past few moments she'd been more afraid of him than anything else.

''Was that Dancing David?'' Sal growled in her ear, and she screamed, clutching a hand to her heart.

"Annie!" Sal laughed, and wrapped his arms around her trembling body. "What on earth is wrong?"

"You scared me," she breathed, flinging her arms around him, trying to shake off her fear. Sal held her at arm's length, letting his eyes travel over her.

He frowned. "What's the matter?"

She shook her head. "Nothing, really. David was just—" She shivered despite the warmth of the summer night.

"What happened? Did he hurt you?"

Annie knew that if she told him David had grabbed her arm, Sal would be livid. "No," she lied. "He just kind of scared me. He gives me the creeps."

"Tell me what happened." Sal's voice was low and threatening and Annie shivered.

"He just stopped by and asked me to get into the car for a minute—I know, Sal. Don't scowl like that. I know you don't like him, but we weren't going anywhere and I thought it would be all right." She shuddered. "He was acting weird. He knows I don't want to go out with him anymore."

"Good." Sal looked at her carefully, his fists bunching at his sides. "Are you sure you're all right?"

She nodded, feeling a great sense of relief knowing Sal was there. "I'm fine."

"Annie," he growled. "I don't want you to see him anymore."

"Sal, I wasn't *seeing* him. He just happened to come by—"

"I don't care what it was. I don't like him, and I don't trust him. I don't want that creep anywhere near you. Now promise me, Annie?"

She looked up at him, her eyes wide and soft. She didn't know if this was some macho declaration of possession, or if Sal was really worried about David.

"Sal?"

His gaze met hers. "What, hon?"

"Is something wrong?"

"Yes," he confirmed with a smile. "You haven't kissed me yet." He bent and nuzzled her mouth with his. Annie forgot her fears and her questions and laced her arms around Sal's neck.

"Kissing in public!" A deep male voice accused, causing Annie to jump back out of Sal's arms. "I tell you, Sal, you never learn. I ought to arrest you for public indecency."

Annie turned, coming face-to-face with a man who would have scared the daylights out of her if he wasn't smiling—and holding a squirming toddler under his arm. He was big, almost as big as Sal, and looked totally intimidating with a shock of pitch-black hair and big, bold blue eyes.

"Ryce!" Sal slapped the man on the shoulder. "How the hell have you been?"

"Busy," Ryce growled, glancing down at the squirming toddler in his arms.

"Michael Ryce, this is Annie Milano." Ryce handed Sal the baby and took Annie's hand.

"It's nice to meet you." He turned to Sal, who was trying to hang on to the squirming child. "I'd say your taste is improving," Ryce said with a grin, flashing Annie a wink.

Annie smiled, immediately liking the man. "And who is this?" Annie asked, taking the baby from Sal. "He's beautiful."

"That," Ryce said proudly, "is Michael Ryce, Junior. And I'll tell his mother you said that."

"How is Willie?" Sal asked, draping an arm around Annie.

"Getting big and crabby. Doctor says it could be twins."

Annie's eyes widened. The child in her arms couldn't be more than a year and a half old. "How many children do you *have*?" she asked in surprise, and Ryce and Sal exchanged amused glances.

"I'll tell you all about it later, Annie," Sal said, draping an arm around her. "But right now, I've got to talk to Ryce."

"Why don't I take the baby inside so you two can talk?" Flashing them a smile, Annie carried the baby inside, letting the door slam shut softly behind her. She'd been a cop's wife long enough to know when to make herself scarce.

"So, did you find out anything?" Sal asked, once Annie was safely inside. Ryce had been Sal's first partner, and Sal had had Ryce, who was now an attorney, do some checking into David and his background.

Ryce shook his dark head. "This Donaldson guy is some interesting character. You sure can pick 'em, Sal."

"He doesn't have a record, I already checked."

Ryce nodded, and smiled. "Hasn't done anything he could get caught at yet. He's into developing residential and commercial property. I found out he's got options on half the land on this block.

Sal frowned. "What do you mean, 'options'?"

"He gave the owners a deposit, so if and when they decide to sell, he gets first crack at a repressed price."

Sal shook his head. "I don't understand. No one in this neighborhood wants to sell. So what's the point in taking an option?"

"What he does, Sal, is take options on properties that he can resell at lucrative prices. The last area he did this in was over in Logan Square. It was a two-block area pretty much like this. Small neighborhood stores, sole proprietors, first- and second-generation Americans who'd lived in the same neighborhood all their lives. No one over there wanted to sell, either."

"So, what happened?"

"I guess there was a rash of burglaries and muggings. The next thing you know, people start to panic. They think the area is unsafe and they want out. Old Donaldson's right there, offering cash on the barrel-head. People are afraid that if they don't sell, they won't be able to get anything for their property, so—"

"So they sell to him at a low price, just to get out." Sal clenched his fists together. "Damn!"

"First one sells, then another, and before you know it, the whole neighborhood changes hands. Donaldson turns around and sells the property to a large developer for ten times what he paid for it."

"That bast—"

"Easy, Sal," Ryce cautioned. "All we've got here is a lot of speculation. We've got no proof that's what he's trying to do here. Or that he was in any way connected with the burglary. But he's scum, Sal, and he uses scare tactics to prey on people's fears.''

''If he comes near Annie again—'' Sal swore under his breath.

''Sal, there's something else you should know.'' Ryce shifted his frame uncomfortably. ''How... uh...fond are you of Annie?'' He'd met a lot of Sal's women over the years, but he'd never seen Sal behave this way about any of them. He had a feeling this lady was special, judging from the look on Sal's face.

''Why?'' Sal asked, curious.

''Well, it seems that Donaldson tries to get to know the people in the neighborhoods. Over in Logan Square he started dating a divorcee; when all hell broke loose, no one suspected him of anything because he'd—''

Sal held up a hand to stop him. ''I get the picture. *Damn!* He's been seeing Annie only to ingratiate himself into the neighborhood so he'll be above suspicion. He's been using Annie to help him carry out his plans.'' Rage ripped through Sal.

Ryce scratched his chin, leaning back against the wall. ''So, uh, if you care about Annie, I suggest you keep her away from this creep.''

''Oh, I will,'' Sal said firmly. ''I will.''

''So, do you?'' Ryce asked, his lips twitching in amusement.

''Do I what?''

''Care about Annie?''

Sal turned to look at his friend and grinned "Yeah."

Ryce shook his head and laughed. "I don't believe it! Finally someone's hooked Smooth, Suave Sal. It's about time. Does she know yet?"

Sal shook his head and stared off down the block. "No," he said quietly. "I've been trying to take things slow. There's a . . . problem," he hedged, and Ryce looked at him carefully.

"Why don't you tell me what the problem is? Maybe I can help."

Sal looked at his friend. Maybe it would do some good to talk to someone about this. He'd carried it around so long, he'd lost all objectivity about it. It sure as hell couldn't hurt. "Do you remember Tony Milano?"

Ryce frowned. "Wasn't he your partner, the one that was killed a couple years ago?" Sal nodded. "Is Annie his—" Sal nodded again.

"Ever since Tony died, I've kind of been looking after Annie. It started out as kind of a friendship, but now—" Sal dragged a hand through his hair "—I've never felt this way about a woman before."

Ryce grinned. He remembered the feeling very well. He'd felt the same way when he had met Willie. "And you're scared."

"That's part of it," Sal acknowledged. "But I also feel guilty."

"What the hell for?"

He sighed. "She was my best friend's wife," Sal said in disgust. "It's like I'm being disloyal to him or something."

"What?" Ryce asked with a frown, trying to understand Sal's problem.

"Hell, Ryce, I'm supposed to be looking out for Annie, not falling in love with her."

"Sal," Ryce said, dropping a hand to his friend's shoulder. "Tony's dead, there's nothing you can do or say to change that. Annie's alive and well. Annie's not his wife, she's his widow. There's a big difference. If you care for her and she cares for you, I don't see what the hell is the problem."

"Ryce," Sal said solemnly. "There's something else."

"What?"

"Do you remember when Tony first died, and I—"

"You borrowed my cabin and took off for a while. Sure, I remember."

"I never told Annie what happened the night Tony died."

Ryce stood perfectly still, waiting. "Do you want to talk about it?"

Sal glanced back over his shoulder, looking through the glass window of the deli. Annie was standing behind the counter, playing with little Michael. His eyes followed her as he began to speak.

"The night Tony died we were supposed to be on a stakeout at a warehouse. We'd gotten a tip that the old Harlem Street gang was back in business and about to hit an electronics warehouse."

"*Supposed* to be?" Ryce questioned. He'd been a cop too long not to pick up on Sal's inflection.

Sal looked at him, his eyes bleak and haunted. "*I* was on the stakeout, but Tony went over to the restaurant, you know the one near the station?"

Ryce nodded, waiting for Sal to go on.

"He wasn't there alone," Sal added softly, taking a deep breath. "Tony was like a brother to me, but I tell you, Ryce, I never approved of the way he acted. But I covered for him, all the time. That night, he'd gone to the restaurant to meet a . . . lady. He was supposed to meet me at ten, but he never showed up. The next thing I know, a call comes over the radio that an officer had been shot—at the restaurant." Sal looked at Ryce, his eyes filled with pain. "By the time I got there, Tony was . . . dead," Sal whispered, his voice tortured.

"What the hell happened?" Ryce growled.

"He was sitting at the table talking to his lady, and I guess her husband came in and caught them. I guess they'd been carrying on for some time, and the husband found out about it. They had words, and the guy pulled a gun."

"God!" Ryce shook his head. "And you mean to say you never told Annie?"

Sal shifted uncomfortably. "I couldn't tell her, Ryce. I covered for Tony, not to protect him, but to protect Annie. I couldn't bear to tell her the truth. It would have killed her. What good would it have done? Tony was dead. What difference did the circumstances make? It wouldn't bring Tony back and it certainly wouldn't change anything. All it would do is hurt her more. And she's had enough of that."

Ryce shook his head again. Now he understood why Sal had been so torn up after his partner's death. "What about Internal Affairs?"

Sal looked at him and smiled sadly. "I know better than to mess around with those guys. I told them the truth. Tony's reputation with the ladies was pretty well-known." Sal shook his head in disgust. "The only one who didn't know about it was Annie."

"You were cleared?"

Sal nodded.

"What did you end up telling Annie?"

"Just that Tony was shot in a restaurant trying to mediate an argument. She received all her benefits because technically Tony was on duty; just because he wasn't where he was supposed to be didn't make any difference. The duty roster showed him on duty, and that's the way they settled it.

"Why the hell didn't you just come clean with her?" Ryce demanded.

"As I said, I didn't want to hurt her. But to tell you the truth, Ryce, by covering up for Tony, even in death, I feel as if I've been just as dishonest and disloyal to Annie as he was." Sal sighed in exasperation. "What the hell am I going to do?"

"Do you love her, Sal?"

Sal was thoughtful for a long moment as his eyes drifted back to Annie. She was nuzzling the baby, with a beautiful smile on her face.

"Do you?" Ryce prompted again, and Sal nodded. "God, yes."

"Then you've got to tell her the truth, Sal, about everything. You've covered for your so-called friend long enough. You've carried this burden long enough. She has a right to know. One thing I know from experience is that you've got to be honest with yourself and your feelings. You've protected this guy long enough, been a better friend than he would have been to you, I'll bet. I have a feeling part of the reason you feel so guilty about your feelings for Annie is because you haven't been honest with her."

Sal looked at Ryce and smiled. "You know, you just might have something there. I hated lying to her; she trusted me. But, hell, I just didn't want to hurt her anymore. I'd planned to tell her, after she'd gotten stronger—but it just never seemed the right time."

"Make the time, Sal. She has a right to know what happened." Ryce snorted in disgust. "Hell, no wonder you took off after Tony was killed. Why the hell didn't you tell me?"

"I just wasn't ready to talk about it, Ryce," he said quietly. "What a waste. Maybe if I'd been there—maybe if I—"

"'Maybe' ain't gonna cut it, Sal," Ryce growled. "Tony was a big boy and knew what he was doing. You've got to stop carrying this guilt around with you. It's not your fault he died. Let the man take responsibility for his own actions. You've been trying to protect a dead man, Sal, and it's tearing you up inside."

Sal watched Annie through the window again; she was smiling as she nuzzled the baby. "How am I going to tell her?"

"Just be up-front about it. Hell, you weren't her husband's keeper. It's going to hurt a hell of a lot more if she finds out from someone else, and believe me, something like that has a way of coming out."

"Hell, Ryce, I waited all my life for Annie. It's right, I just know it. But I'm afraid if I tell her—if she learns I've deliberately deceived her—I don't want to lose her. For the first time in my life, I'm scared."

Ryce smiled. "Scared? Hell, Sal, you're not the first man love has crept up on and taken by surprise. It's scary. But you owe it to her and to yourself to be honest. It's the only way for you two to begin anew." Ryce clapped Sal on the shoulder. "Just tell her. Everything. I have a feeling once you come clean with her, all your guilt will disappear."

"I just don't want to hurt her, she's had enough hurt to last her a lifetime."

"Make no mistake, Sal, it's not going to be easy. She's going to be hurt. But once she realizes why you did what you did, and how much you love her, she'll understand."

Sal sighed. "I hope so, Ryce. I hope so." Sal smiled. "Thanks, Ryce. I appreciate it."

Ryce laughed. "Appreciate it, hell. Wait until I tell Willie someone has finally captured Smooth, Suave Sal!"

Chapter Eight

Ryce seems very nice, but a little intimidating," Annie said with a laugh as she pushed her plate away. She glanced around the small restaurant. Nestled in the basement of a converted brownstone, Parillo's was a family-run operation and had the best Italian food in the city. The decor was strictly cafeteria, red-and-white plastic tablecloths, vinyl-covered chairs, and fake flowers strewn about the walls. Loud Italian music blared from speakers hoisted near the ceilings. What Parillo's lacked in decor, it made up for in cuisine. The place was known citywide for its food and was packed almost every night. She brought her gaze back to Sal's, her eyes sparkling.

He laughed softly, covering her hand with his. "Ryce has been called a lot worse things than just intimidating, Annie. But he's a great guy. Since he fell in love with Willie, he's really changed."

"You promised to tell me the rest of the story," she reminded him, anxious to hear more.

Smiling, Sal sipped his coffee. "T.C. was a street-smart eleven-year-old hell-bent and headed for trouble. Until he ran into Ryce. Boy, Annie, that kid didn't know the meaning of the word *trouble* until he met Ryce. They were two of a kind—unorthodox, rebellious, loners. Ryce lived by his own rules, cop or not. When he met T.C., Ryce was determined to give the kid a home, and something else he never had—love. But Willie—that's Ryce's wife, she was the social worker in charge of T.C. She took one look at Ryce and decided he wasn't suited to raise a flag, let alone a child. For a while, things between the two of them flew fast and furious, with Willie and Ryce colliding at every turn. But eventually they worked it out. And somewhere along the line, Ryce, the guy who never let anyone close, fell head over heels in love with Willie." Sal laughed. "It's hard to believe he's actually married and the father of five."

"Five!" Annie gasped.

"T.C. was the first kid they took in. Somehow, over the past two years, Ryce has brought home three more, as well as their having had Michael Ryce, Junior."

"And his wife's expecting again?" Annie's eyes glittered with amazement, and just a bit of envy. She'd always wanted children, but Tony had been violently opposed to the idea, fearing it would tie them down.

Sal nodded. "Twins, Ryce said. He was the last guy in the world I ever expected to get married."

"Kind of like you," she teased, and Sal's eyes darkened.

"Annie," he said quietly, his eyes softly searching hers. He covered her hand with his. He wanted so much to tell her what he was feeling, but he knew he couldn't until they'd settled a few things. He'd been trying so hard the past few weeks to prove to her that what was happening between them was not just some emotional tie, or a feeling of duty or obligation, but the real thing.

She filled his nights and his days. All he could do was think about Annie. Soon he would tell her, but he wanted to be sure she understood that this was something precious between them. Love didn't come too often, at least not the kind of love he felt for her. He wanted to take his time, let her get used to the idea. He'd waited his whole life for her, and Sal knew if he had to, he could wait a little more. She was worth it.

"Annie," he said slowly, gently stroking her hand with his thumb, loving the instant response she gave. "I've never gotten married because I haven't found the right woman. Marriage is too important to make a mistake. When I get married, it's going to be forever."

Forever. Her eyes slid closed and Annie desperately clung to her composure. She couldn't read anything into Sal's comments. She couldn't get her hopes up. But still, the thought of being married to Sal, of having his children, brought a wonderful giddiness to her heart.

"Come on. Let's go back to your house. You can walk off some of that wine," he said with a grin. Sal stood up, dropped his napkin to the table and pulled her chair out.

Nodding, Annie let Sal guide her out of the restaurant, feeling a bit woozy. Usually a nondrinker, she'd had two glasses of wine and they'd gone immediately to her head.

Breathing deeply of the warm night air, Annie sighed happily as they walked. Parillo's was only a few blocks from her house and they'd chosen to walk, and enjoy the warm summer evening. She glanced at Sal, noting he was watching her intently, a strange expression on his face.

Something was on his mind. Something important. She'd known him long enough to know his moods. He shared everything with her, and she knew when he was ready, he would talk to her.

Sal clasped her hand in his. "Let's walk to Peanut Park." Peanut Park was really officially named Arrigo Park, but renamed Peanut because of its unusual shape. Bordered by saplings and cottonwoods, the park was nearly deserted except for a few children playing stickball at the north end.

Holding hands, they walked in silence for a few moments, occasionally waving to a neighbor who was still sitting outside.

"Annie?"

"What, Sal?"

He stopped, turning to face her directly. "Do you ever think about…him?" He tightened his fingers on her hand as his gaze held hers.

She didn't need to ask who he was talking about. She knew. *Tony.* It was odd for Sal to bring him up now, after all this time. Sal had never talked about him. In fact, he'd deliberately avoided talking about him. Perhaps that explained his sudden quietness.

"Sometimes," she admitted.

"What do you think about?" he asked quietly, urging her forward. Sal carefully held her arm as they avoided a broken patch in the sidewalk.

Annie thought about his question. "I don't know, I guess I think about what a waste it was for him to die so young. I think about—I guess I think about a lot of things. After Tony first—after it first happened, I thought a lot about him." She shrugged. "I guess I felt guilty."

"Guilty?" Sal came to a halt directly under a streetlamp and looked at her. "What the hell did you have to feel guilty about?"

Annie glanced away. This was something—her innermost feelings about her husband—that she'd never discussed with anyone. She wasn't certain anyone would understand.

"Well," she said tentatively, "I think about the fact that our marriage . . . well, it never really had a chance to get off the ground." A flash of lightning lit up the sky.

"Let's head back, before we get caught in a downpour," Sal suggested, wondering about her statement. He guided her back in the direction of the house. A breeze kicked up, ruffling the trees. Annie pushed a tumbled curl off her face.

"Do you miss him?" Sal asked carefully, picking up the conversation. Annie smiled in the darkness.

"Sometimes—I guess." She sighed, keeping her gaze downcast. "It all seems so long ago. When I think about him now, it seems as if we really weren't married at all.''

"Why?" He glanced at her, his eyes roaming over her beautiful features. Her curls had come loose from the combs she'd secured them with, and now blew around her face like a dark halo.

Annie shrugged. It was going to be hard to put what she wanted to say into words. "Tony and I—" She stopped. "It's been so long now, Sal. Memories fade," she said softly. She'd never talked to anyone about the problems in her marriage. There was never anyone to talk about them *with*. Tony could be very noncommunicative. There would be periods of time when he didn't talk to her at all, about anything. It was hard to admit, even to Sal, that her so-called perfect marriage wasn't so perfect after all.

Sal was so different from Tony. She could talk to him about anything. He was easygoing and even tempered. She couldn't ever remember Sal really losing his temper, or going into a black mood. It was hard to believe at times that he and Tony had been friends all their lives. They were so different.

"Does it bother you to talk about him?" Sal asked gently, giving her hand an encouraging squeeze.

Annie shivered a bit as the night breeze turned cooler. Goose bumps rose along her bare arms, and Sal instinctively draped an arm around her shoulder, drawing her closer to his warmth. "No," she said hesitantly. "It's just . . . some things I've just never discussed with anyone."

"I know the feeling," Sal muttered.

She struggled to pick up the thread of their conversation as Sal steered her around a corner toward her house. She took a deep breath. "Tony was reclusive at times. I was married to him but sometimes I felt as if I didn't really know him. I know that sounds strange, but—"

"No, Annie," Sal said softly. "I understand." He led her up the stairs and sank down on the top step, pulling her with him. He put his arm around her shoulder. "Go on," he urged.

"I don't know, Sal. I always thought marriage would be different from what it was."

"Were you disappointed?" He saw the hesitation in her eyes, and wrapped his arms around her, pulling her close, cradling her against him. "Were you?" he repeated softly.

Annie swallowed hard. "Yes," she admitted. "And I feel terribly guilty even saying that." She smiled sadly. "Marriage wasn't quite what I expected—at least, marriage to Tony." Her voice dropped, and she glanced away. "Tony proposed right after my father died. It was a rough time for me. My mother had only been gone two years and I suddenly realized how alone I was." Annie stared off into the distance, remembering the pain she'd felt at the time. "I loved Tony, but sometimes I felt so lonely when we were married. We didn't really share a lot of things. It was almost as if we were just two people living in the same house, with nothing else tying us together. Can you understand that?" She glanced at him, wondering how he would take her comments. Sal nodded.

He understood it all too well. "Do you think you'd ever want to get married again?" He stared at her a moment, his expression serious, his dark eyes probing. Annie shifted nervously under his scrutiny.

"Sometimes I think about it," she admitted, smiling softly, unwilling to add that the only person she'd ever thought about marrying was him. "But the next time—if there is a next time—I wouldn't settle for being shut out." She lifted her chin and met his gaze. "If I ever get married again, Sal, it would have to be to someone who would share everything with me. I don't ever want to feel like I'm giving one hundred percent and only getting ten percent in return. I want a marriage that's equal. I want to know that I'm as important to my husband as he would be to me." She chuckled softly. "I know, to a confirmed bachelor like you it probably sounds like a life sentence."

"No, not at all," he said quietly, absently stroking circles on her bare shoulder. "It sounds...wonderful. Even confirmed bachelors think about marriage once in a while." The thought of giving all of that to her, and then getting it in return sounded like heaven. Sal smiled inwardly, wondering if she knew how delectable she looked.

"Not you, Sal. I can't imagine you settling down with just one woman." Annie laughed softly, the tension leaving her as his fingers lulled her into sensuous slumber. Her eyes slid closed on a heavy sigh as Annie laid her head on his shoulder, tired now from the wine and the food.

"Maybe I just haven't found the right woman yet," he countered, leisurely stroking her arm and shoulder. Her breath came unsteadily as her heart responded to his nearness.

"That's just what your mother said." Sighing contentedly, Annie buried her face close to the warmth of his neck.

"Surely an unimpeachable, impartial source," he teased, kissing the top of her head.

"Sal?"

"Hmm?"

"Do...do...*you* ever think about him?"

His hand stilled on her shoulder, and she lifted her head to look into his eyes. "Sometimes," he admitted, urging her head back down on to his chest. Absently he stroked her hair, wanting to protect her from what he had to tell her.

"What do you think about?" she asked softly.

"Oh, I don't know," he said with a sigh. "A lot of things, I guess." His voice was gentle, but she thought she detected a hint of sadness.

Sal sighed. How could he explain to her that missing Tony wasn't the problem. The problem was coming to terms with what he had to tell her. He'd done a lot of thinking tonight, and he realized that what Ryce had said was true. He'd been protecting Tony—at his own expense and Annie's. Ryce was right. She had a right to know the truth about what had happened.

Maybe he'd been wrong in keeping it from her, but at the time he'd thought he was doing what was best for her. He'd seen no point in hurting her any further, and he'd known that she would have been devastated.

It had been two years now; hopefully the pain had dulled. And she had him and his love to help her over the rough spots. But he couldn't help but wonder if it would be enough.

They couldn't have any kind of relationship unless they were truthful with one another. Annie had had enough deceptions from the men in her life; she deserved the truth. He just didn't know quite how he was going to tell her.

"You miss him, don't you?" Annie asked, wondering why he was so quiet. She knew Sal didn't like to talk about Tony. It was the one and only thing he'd never discussed with her. She understood. Some things were too painful. She often wondered if perhaps Sal relived the night of Tony's death over and over every time he talked about it.

"Sometimes. He was my best friend, Annie, and Tony and I knew each other our whole lives; but that doesn't mean I approved of everything he did. From the time we were little, I covered for him. No matter what, I always covered his rear. Tony wasn't a bad guy, he just never really grew up. In a lot of ways, he was still very immature."

Another crack of thunder split the sky. Annie nodded, burrowing closer to his warmth. "Do you think..." She paused. "Sal, do you think it's terrible for us to talk like this... about him?"

"No, Annie, not terrible. I think it's about time. You know, it's one of the few things we've never really discussed."

"I know," she said softly. "I always felt like it was the one thing you didn't want to talk about. I just thought it was too painful. I knew you had to deal with it in your own way."

Sal knew she was referring to the fact that he'd gone off to Ryce's cabin in the need to be alone. But it wasn't Tony's death he'd had to deal with, so much as the lies. He hadn't liked it any more then than he liked it now. But he'd done it for Annie. Would she understand that?

Annie took a deep breath as Sal tightened his arms around her, drawing her even closer. It felt so right, so natural to be here in his arms.

She didn't care what the reasons were for his always being around, for his always being here for her. Obligation, loyalty—she didn't care what the reason. At the moment the reasons didn't matter. All that mattered was he was here with her. For now, that was enough.

Sal was a very special person, a very special man. And Annie was just glad she had him as a friend. If that's all he would ever be to her, she would enjoy him and the time she had with him and be grateful for that.

"Annie," he said, his eyes twinkling. "I think there's something else we should talk about?"

"Mmm, what, Sal?" she asked drowsily.

"Us, Annie," Sal said softly, and Annie stiffened.

"Us?" she repeated, drawing back and out of his arms to search his face. "As in you and me, us?"

He ruffled her hair. "Don't look so shocked. We've successfully avoided talking about what's been happening between us, and I don't want to do that anymore. I want things to be out in the open."

"Sal," she protested, lifting a hand to stroke his face. "You've always been open and honest with me. You were always the one person in the world I knew I could trust, could count on." Her generous mouth tilted and Sal's heart constricted. She was looking up at him with such hope, such trust. God! She was going to be devastated when she learned that not only had her husband betrayed her, but in his own way, so had he.

"Annie, things have changed between us. It's got nothing to do with bonding or attachments or chaperoning, or anything else for that matter."

She nodded, her heart pounding in hope. She loved the feel of being so close to him, having him near, even if it did make her pulse thud and her knees weak.

"Annie, I know you think I've just been hanging around out of some sense of obligation or duty. I don't know, maybe it started out that way. After Tony died, you just seemed so lost, so alone."

"I *was* lost, and alone. Sal, you have to realize, at the time I felt like I'd lost everything, and everyone who cared about me. My mother, father and my husband all died within three years." She blinked back tears, remembering how alone she'd felt. It was a frightening feeling, knowing that you had no one to turn to, no one to share things with. "And then you came to the rescue—" she laughed softly "—my knight in shining armor." She touched his face again, loving its gritty texture. "You always knew just the right thing to do, the right thing to say. You made me feel so much better about myself, about everything." Her eyes held his. "Whenever I needed you, no matter what the reason, I knew I could always count on you. I never felt quite so alone when you were around."

Sal smiled, and Annie paused to take a deep breath. "But you don't have to worry about me anymore, Sal. I'm not going to go out with David anymore—or anyone like him."

"You bet you're not," he growled, not liking the direction this conversation was taking. He turned her around to look at her, his eyes lovingly tracing her features."

"Oh, Sal," she murmured, leaning her head against his shoulder. "What would I do without you?"

"Let's hope you never have to find out," he whispered, wrapping his arms around her. Annie sighed deeply, not wanting to sort through the complications of all her emotions.

"So Annie, tell me, what do you think of this dating stuff?" His mouth twitched in humor. "I know I haven't taken you to any fancy-pants places, but have you been having a good time?"

She laughed, surprised that he would be concerned. "No maybe about it, Sal." He looked at her and she saw the uncertainty in his eyes. "I definitely had a good time. I always have a good time with you," she admitted truthfully, and he grinned.

"Does that mean we can make this a habit?"

"It does," she assured him.

"Annie?"

"What, Sal?"

He reached out, lacing his fingers through hers. Gently he caressed her silky skin with his thumb, sending heated tremors of delight through her. "Annie," he said, his voice deep and quiet, drawing her gaze to his. "I want to kiss you." He leaned forward, brushing his lips gently across hers, testing for acceptance.

With a sigh of pleasure, Annie slipped her arms around him, leaning into him and welcoming his touch. Her heart filled with love for him, and Annie knew it that instant: what she felt wasn't attachment or friendship, or anything else but love.

The thought left her reeling. She loved Sal. *She loved him*, but not as a friend, the way he loved her. She loved Sal the way a woman loves a man. With her heart and her soul and everything within her.

Angling his head, he settled his lips firmly over hers. Her senses thrilled in delight and she caressed him in turn, gently stroking his broad back and shoulders.

She clung to him, whimpering softly at the yearning he awakened in her. His mouth moved relentlessly over hers, possessive and demanding. There was nothing friendly about his kiss. It was purely male, filling her with a need so strong she felt the world spin.

His soft tongue teased her, demanding she respond in kind. Shyly Annie followed his lead, doing as he did and enjoying the sensations he aroused in her. Her breathing came fast, heavily, causing her breasts to rise and fall against his chest. She felt her heart slam against her ribs as he slowly traced the length of her spine.

"Annie," he breathed, pulling his mouth free. There was a huskiness in his voice she hadn't heard before. The rapid rate of his breathing matched her own. "You are so beautiful," he groaned, dropping his lips to her neck to nip at the soft skin of her throat.

Her head fell back with abandon, and Annie moaned softly as Sal planted feather-light kisses up her neck, capturing the lobe of her ear in his mouth.

"Annie." He pressed his lips gently to her temple, rubbing his hands up and down her slender back. She began to tremble, knowing if she didn't pull away, Sal would see the love in her eyes, feel the need in her body. She didn't want that.

"I'd better go—" Annie froze as the sound of glass shattering splintered the night air. She could hear loud voices and someone—several someones—running. "Sal?" She turned to him, her eyes wide with fright. "The deli," she whispered, clutching his arm.

Sal jumped to his feet, checking his gun. He scooped his suit coat off the step and tugged her to her feet. "Go in the house, Annie," he ordered, shoving the jacket in her direction and pushing her toward the door.

"But Sal—" She began to tremble.

"Go in and lock the door," he ordered. "And don't open it until I come back. Do you understand?" Annie nodded, her eyes widened in fear.

"Go!"

Clutching his suit jacket in her arms, Annie turned and bolted into the house, slamming it shut soundly behind her. Heaving a deep breath, she went to the window. Sal was gone. All she could see were the faint drops of rain that splattered against the pane. Hugging his jacket close, Annie sank down on a chair to wait.

Chapter Nine

Annie paced the floors, waiting and worrying as the hours ticked by. What on earth had happened? Where was Sal? A hand of panic settled around her heart, making her throat tighten and burn. She had a feeling something was terribly wrong.

Oh, Lord. Annie blindly went from room to room, trying not to worry.

Sal, where are you?

Terror washed over her and she pressed her fingers to her tired eyes, wanting to stop her tortured thoughts. If something happened to him—Lord, she couldn't go through this—not again. She'd already been through it once, and once was more than enough for any woman.

Despite Tony's death, until tonight Annie had never given much thought to the danger Sal faced every day. It wasn't something she thought about; it was a fact of life in his job—a job he loved. He dealt with danger, life and death every day. He knew it was there, but he never talked about it, never expressed any concern.

Once she'd asked him about it—asked him if he'd ever been scared, or if he was more careful now because of what had happened to Tony. She remembered Sal had smiled sadly, saying a careful cop was the one who usually got himself in trouble. When you started thinking too much, you started second-guessing yourself and being careful instead of relying on instinct and training, and that's when you got yourself trouble. That was the time to be scared.

Heaving a short, tension-filled sigh, Annie went into the kitchen, then promptly forgot what she'd gone in there for. Standing in the middle of the room, she sighed, then went back into the living room to wait.

"Be careful," she whispered, pressing her nose to the damp glass. "No, don't be careful," she corrected, scanning the darkened street. *"Be smart."*

She'd just found love—again. She hadn't even had a chance to tell him, and now she might lose it—again.

The rain finally stopped, and the darkness slid into dawn, leaving a dull, damp ache in her heart and a weariness in her breast.

Why didn't he call? *Maybe he couldn't call.*

Why didn't he come back? *Maybe he couldn't come back.*

"Stop this, Annie," she scolded herself aloud, knowing she was more worried than she thought if she'd started talking to herself.

She finally went into her bedroom, dragged a blue quilted comforter off the bed, pulled the rocker up to the window and curled up in it. She buried her nose in the quilt, loving the warm softness of it. Sal had given it to her for her birthday, and she loved the intricate wedding-ring pattern.

During that first long, cold winter, when she was so alone and so lonely, she would take the quilt and wrap herself up in it like a child. For some reason, the quilt always brought a sense of comfort, something she sorely needed right now.

Time slipped by, and weariness overtook her. Her head drooped and her lashes lowered. She rocked more slowly, finally allowing her eyes to close.

The bell rang. And rang. Startled, Annie jumped up, nearly tripping over her feet and the comforter. Bundling it up around her, she hurried to the front door and froze.

There was a blue-and-white squad car parked in front of her house. Her heart slowed. Oh, God. For a moment she froze in fear, remembering another night when a squad car had pulled up to the door.

Her lashes slid closed and she said a quick, silent prayer, holding on to a sliver of hope. She unlocked the door and flung it open just as the officer was getting back into the car.

He turned, and she recognized Rich Vesto. The breath slipped out of her in a rush. Rich was a neighbor. He lived right around the corner from the deli and he and his wife Maria were frequent customers. Annie stood staring at him, unable to open her mouth, her heart pounding in fear.

"Hi, Annie," Rich called, smiling as he slammed the car door and turned back up the walk toward her. "Sal asked me to stop by—"

"Sal?" She sagged against the door, letting her breath come. He was alive. "Is…is he all right?" She opened the door wider, ushering Rich in.

"He's fine, Annie. I was on my way home and he asked me to drop by and let you know he was all right. He also asked me to check the deli. Guess he picked up a couple of kids for breaking the windows again. I just went by, the board-up company's already been there, so you don't have to worry."

Sal was fine. She gave silent thanks, suddenly not caring about broken windows or the deli, or anything else. "Where is he?"

Rich took his hat off. "At the station." He scratched his bald head. "I guess those kids are the key to something he's been working on. Said to tell you he'll stop by as soon as he's done."

She smiled, leaning up to kiss his cheek in a gesture of great relief. "Thanks, Rich. Stop by the deli for lunch tomorrow. I'll have Rosina make you one of her special sandwiches, on the house."

He grinned sheepishly. "Can't pass up an offer like that." He patted his stomach. "You know how I love Rosina's sandwiches. Almost as much as my Maria's cooking."

"How *is* Maria?" Annie asked with a smile.

Rich beamed. "Fine, just fine. Twenty years and we're still going strong." He twisted his hat in his hands. "You know, Annie, everyone in the neighborhood—well—we're all glad to see you and Sal—" He twisted his hat nervously. "You deserve some happiness after what happened with Tony. None of us approved of the things he did, we thought you deserved better."

Annie frowned in confusion. "What did Tony do, Rich?"

Rich paled. "Well, I'd better say good-night, Maria is waiting." With a tip of his hat he was gone, leaving Annie standing in the doorway staring after him, his words ringing in her ears.

What did he mean, *none of us approved of the things Tony did*? What things? Confused, Annie shut the door and relocked it, gathering the comforter around her and going back to sit in the rocker. She thought about Rich's statements for a long time, wondering just what he meant.

Tucking her feet under her, Annie sighed softly and closed her eyes. As her lashes drooped, she made a mental note to ask Sal about it. All she could think about now was that he was safe.

"Annie." Someone was gently shaking her, and her eyes flew open.

"Sal!" she breathed, struggling to wake up and sit up at the same time. "My, God!" She reached up and touched his bruised face. "What happened to you?"

Sal tried to smile, but it came out a wince. "If you think I look bad, you should see Dancing David." His lip was split and he had one hell of a shiner.

"David!" Annie said in alarm, wondering what the devil was going on. Now wasn't the time to ask. Sal looked as if he were about to fall over. Annie scrambled out of her rocker. "Come on," she said, taking his arm and guiding him across the room. She tried to ease some of his weight as he sank down heavily on the couch, holding his left side and groaning. "Are you hurt?" she inquired, kneeling next to him. Her eyes went over him and he smiled—or tried to. Of course he was hurt!

"I ... mean ... how badly are you hurt? What happened?" Her words came tumbling out in a rush, spilling out of her mouth in a flurry as she tried to take his shoes off. His clothes were still damp from the rain, and his hair was plastered across his bruised forehead. Lord, she couldn't let him go home like this. She had to keep Sal here until she was certain he was all right.

"Annie." He lifted a hand and stroked her cheek. "I'm fine," he assured her, his eyes hinting at mischief despite his pain. "I just want to rest for a moment, then I'll go home. I didn't want you to worry. Did Rich stop by?"

She nodded, her voice filled with worry. "Let me clean your face." She hurried into the kitchen to get a pan with clean water. Grabbing some cotton and some antiseptic from a cabinet, Annie hurried back into the living room to find Sal stretched out on the couch, his eyes closed.

She knelt down beside him, gently rinsing the rag and dabbing at his wounds. Her breath caught when he winced as she found a particularly sore spot under his eye.

"It's not so bad," he assured her. "Looks worse than it is."

"I'll bet," she murmured, lifting his feet to a more comfortable position on the couch and then covering him with the comforter. "Rest, Sal," she instructed, gently touching his face.

"We have to talk," he murmured drowsily. She nodded. Her eyes went over him again. She wanted to soothe away each cut, each bruise. Her heart constricted in pain.

"What happened?" she whispered as Sal shifted his weight, moaning softly.

"After I left last night, I chased a couple of guys—kids, really. The glass we heard breaking was the deli window. Don't worry, now," he said, touching a finger to her cheek. "I just stopped by there and the board-up company has already been there. There's not much they can do about the spray paint—"

Her hands stilled on his face. "Spray paint!"

Sal slowly nodded. "They painted all over the brick before they broke all the windows. They'd just taken off when I rounded the corner. They made the mistake of cutting through Peanut Park." He grinned. "I cut them off at the pass. I wanted to wring each one of their necks, Annie. But they were just kids, no more than fifteen or sixteen." Sal groaned as she wiped at his cheek. "I knew damn well they weren't working on their own. They were scared to death. I took them down to the station and they spilled their guts. Dancing David was behind all of it."

"David!" Annie frowned. "Sal, I don't understand. Why on earth would David want to vandalize the deli? This doesn't make any sense."

"Annie, listen to me," he said gently. "He's been trying to scare you into selling the store."

"What!" Annie laughed and shook her head. "What on earth would he want with a little deli? He hates this neighborhood and everyone in it. This doesn't make any sense."

"It's not the deli he wants, Annie; it's the land it's on. He knows neither you nor the neighbors want to sell. The last time he did something like this, a rash of burglaries and muggings occurred and people got scared. They decided to sell out before things got too bad and good ole Davey was right there with the cash. The people took the little pittance he offered because they were afraid if they didn't, they wouldn't be able to get anything for their property. Davey then resold the property to a developer at an enormous profit. Ryce found out David has already paid some of your neighbors money for an option on their property. The money is kind of like his insurance policy. If they ever decide to sell, he gets first crack."

"But, Sal, he hasn't paid *me* any money, and he knows I have no intention of selling." She gently dabbed at his face, aching inside for the pain he had.

"I know, hon, but this isn't the first time he's tried to scare someone into selling. That's why he's been hanging around—"

"Sal," she said slowly. "Are you saying David was ... using me?" Her face flamed in horror as she realized what a fool she'd been.

"Honey, now don't get upset," Sal cautioned gently. "I suspected it right from the beginning. There was just something about him that rubbed me the wrong way."

"Sal, wait a minute, are you saying you knew about this all along?" No wonder he thought she needed a chaperon! "How long have you suspected David was behind all of this?" she asked, suddenly confused. If Sal had known about this, or suspected David right from the beginning, why hadn't he told her? Why on earth would he keep something like that from her?

"Right from that first night," he admitted, and Annie's heart slowly began to ache. If Sal had suspected David right from the beginning, then... She looked at him carefully, feeling an overwhelming sense of dread.

"Without proof there wasn't much I could do. That's why I wanted to keep an eye on him. That first night after the burglary, I had my suspicions, but I couldn't very well charge him with anything since he had an ironclad alibi. You and I were with him all evening, and I sure didn't want to have to try and explain *that* to a judge. I knew if my hunch was right, it was just a matter of time until he showed his true colors. Even my mother and aunt were suspicious of him."

Oh, Lord, Annie thought. No wonder Florina and Rosina got so upset every time David showed up. Everyone knew about this but her. How could she have been so naive?

"Is that why you didn't want me to date him anymore, because you suspected he was behind all the trouble I've been having?" Annie tried to brace herself for his answer.

"Part of it," Sal admitted, and Annie felt her temper erupt. All this time she'd thought Sal was interested in *her*! He didn't care about her or the deli; all Sal cared about was getting the goods on David!

What a fool she'd been. The walls of her heart ached with a pain that went straight to her soul. Why hadn't she realized? Why had she let her imagination run away with her? She'd been a blind, romantic fool. She should have known Sal wasn't the type of man to be interested in only one woman. How could she not have realized what he was doing? Sal was still trying to protect her, still watching over her. But she didn't want his protection; what she wanted was his love.

"I knew sooner or later we'd get him," Sal went on. "You know what they say, slime always rises to the top. Once the boys were in custody and they confessed David had paid them fifty bucks apiece to burglarize and then vandalize the deli, I knew we had him. But I still needed concrete proof. It was his word against two kids who were admitted thieves. After they took care of the deli they were supposed to meet David. I followed them and watched the payoff. I also heard his instructions as to what to do tomorrow."

"Tomorrow? How far did he plan to carry this thing?"

Sal's eyes darkened. "Don't ask, Annie," he cautioned, shuddering at the memory. Just the thought of what David had planned to do to Annie caused his guts to tighten. "Just don't ask. I arrested him right then and there."

"And?" she prompted, still wondering where the fight came in.

Sal grinned. "Let's just say David resisted arrest."

"Why didn't you tell me about this?" she demanded.

"I didn't want to frighten you."

"Frighten me!" Annie cried furiously. "I'm not a child, Sal!"

"I know, hon," Sal said softly. "But I didn't want you to worry, at least not until I had some proof."

She stood up on shaky legs. "You should have told me the truth," she accused, knowing that if he had, she would never have allowed herself to fall in love with him. But now it was too late. She wasn't the kind of woman to turn her feelings on and off like a faucet. She'd fallen totally and helplessly in love with him, constantly holding on to the hope that someday he might feel the same way. Now she knew it was never to be.

Sal looked at Annie carefully, noting the sudden paleness of her skin. "Annie, I told you I didn't want to worry or frighten you. I knew the situation was under control. Every time David showed up, I made sure someone called me."

Her eyes slid closed and a wave of pain rocked her. Oh, Lord, it was worse than she'd thought. The whole *neighborhood* knew what a fool she'd been. Poor Annie, the little widow woman who couldn't even tell when a man was using her.

"Sal! How could you do that?" she cried. "I must look like an incompetent fool who can't even take care of herself!"

Sal sat up. "No, Annie, that's not the way it looks. How on earth were you supposed to know what David was up to? What good would it have done to tell you, anyway? You were frightened enough by the burglary as it was. I didn't think there was any point in worrying you any further.''

"You didn't think—'' She dashed at her tears of humiliation that slid down her cheeks. ''Sal, when are you going to realize I'm a big girl and I don't need your protection?'' How dare he treat her like a six-year-old child who needed to be watched over constantly.

"Annie, that's not the way— Hon,'' Sal said, rising up on one elbow and trying to calm her down. ''I only did it to protect you.''

"Sal, I don't need your protection,'' she protested, knowing it was a lie. She needed Sal more than she'd ever needed anything in her life. ''What else haven't you told me?'' Annie demanded.

His eyes darkened and a muscle along his temple jumped. She knew immediately there was more that he wasn't telling.

"What else?'' she demanded and Sal sighed.

Tell her the truth. Be up-front. She has a right to know. Ryce's words echoed in Sal's mind, and he knew what he had to do. He loved Annie more than anything in the world, but they could never have a real relationship unless he was honest with her. Even though he'd tried so hard to protect her all this time, she was right. She was a big girl, and she had a right to know. If only he could take away some of the pain. He shouldn't have kept anything from her. Not the information about David, and definitely not the truth about the way Tony died. Would she understand that he had done it out of love and not malice? He hoped so. He was betting his future happiness on it.

"Annie, come sit down," he said gently, reaching out his hand to her.

She avoided his hand but sat down on the couch next to him, wondering what else he'd been trying to protect her from.

"I want to talk to you about the night Tony died," Sal said quietly, and her eyes flew to his.

"What does Tony's death have to do with all of this?" she asked in confusion.

Sal was silent for a long moment. He took her hand, holding it tenderly. "Nothing, but there's something I've never told you about that night."

Annie felt herself stiffen. "What do you mean?"

"What I mean is I just couldn't bring myself to tell you the truth about what happened," he said quietly.

Annie looked at him carefully. "What happened that night, Sal?" she asked, her eyes searching his. A band of pressure tightened around her heart.

"Tony and I were supposed to be on a stakeout. Tony decided to go over to the restaurant; you know, the one by the station."

"What on earth was he doing there if he was supposed to be on a stakeout?" Her eyes searched his for some clue, but all she saw was a haunting sadness that caused her throat to constrict. "Sal?"

"Annie," he said softly, laying a hand on her arm. "Tony was with another woman."

"W-what?" Her eyes searched his, praying this was all a mistake.

"Tony had been seeing her for a while, and I guess her husband found out. He found them together that night. They had words and the next thing I knew..." His voice trailed off and he reached out to her, but she shrank away from him.

"Oh, God," she whispered, pushing herself to her feet. Tears welled in her eyes as she paced the floor, trying to digest it all.

All this time she'd thought her husband... Oh, God. No wonder Sal could never talk to her about that night. It wasn't because it hurt him to talk about Tony's death, but because he was covering for him. All this time Sal had been lying to her. And she'd never questioned him—about anything. She'd just believed everything he said as if it were etched in stone.

"All this time," she whispered. "You've been lying to me... about Tony, about his death, about everything."

The look in her eyes caused Sal's heart to crumble in anguish. He shot to his feet and went to her. "No, Annie, I didn't lie to you about everything. I just didn't see any point in telling you the specific circumstances. Tony was dead; what good would it have done? I saw the look on your face the night he died, remember? *I* was the one who had to tell you. I knew then I couldn't bring myself to inflict any more pain on you. Annie, I'm sorry, I never meant to hurt you or mislead you. I was only trying to protect you."

"Protect me!" she cried. "You sure cover a lot of ground with those two little words, Sal. I trusted you," she said in disbelief, whirling away from him.

"I thought you were my friend, the one person left in the world I could count on."

He grabbed her shoulders and turned her to face him. But she refused to look at him. "You can trust me, Annie, and you can count on me."

She laughed softly—a thin, hysterical sound that Sal felt clear through to his bones. "You've been deceiving me for two years, Sal; I'd hardly say that's a basis for trust." She wanted to cry, to strike out at him for what he'd done to her. A sob caught in her throat and she whirled away from him again, not wanting him to see her pain.

"Annie, please, don't. Let me explain."

"Explain!" She blinked away the tears that filled her eyes. "What else have you lied to me about, Sal?" Her eyes were huge and dark with the pain of betrayal and he felt his heart constrict.

"Nothing, Annie. I've never lied to you about anything but this." Sal had never known a pain such as he felt at this moment. He wanted to pull her into his arms, hold her and protect her from the pain that racked her body.

"You expect me to believe you?" she asked incredulously. "I trusted you," she whispered. "I never thought you'd lie to me about—about—anything." She raised her stricken eyes to his. "Why?" she breathed, desperate to know why and how he could do this to her.

"What good would it have done to tell you? He was gone and nothing could bring him back. What difference did it make—"

"'Difference'?" She dashed at the tears that slid down her cheeks. "You don't understand, do you? It makes a great deal of difference, Sal. How could you keep something like that from me?"

"Don't you think you'd been through enough, Annie? Please, listen to me."

"No," she whispered, shrugging off his hands. "Don't touch me—please, Sal, just leave me alone."

He knew he had to make her understand. He did what he did because he loved her and cared about her, not because he wanted to hurt her or betray her. Sal knew that if he didn't reach her now, if he didn't make her understand, he might lose her. And he couldn't bear the thought. He'd waited his whole life for her—for love—and he wasn't about to lose her now.

"Annie, please?"

"No," she whispered, unable to turn and face him. "Please, Sal, I just want you to leave. I need . . . some time to think." Her voice broke and her control slipped another notch as Rich's words came flooding back. *You deserve a better husband than Tony was.* So this, too, was something else everyone in the neighborhood knew about but her. No wonder Sal thought she needed a chaperon!

A sob tore loose from her throat. "Sal, please leave me alone. Just go."

Sal stood there for a moment. His heart and his arms ached for her, and once again he cursed his childhood friend for all the pain he had caused them all.

"I'll go, Annie," he said. "But I'll be back. You can count on it." Sal turned on his heel and headed for the door.

You can count on it. At one time, she'd been certain Sal was the only thing she could count on. Now she knew differently. There wasn't anything or anyone she could count on but herself.

The soft click of the door shutting behind him opened up the dam of tears Annie had been holding inside. Wrapping her arms around herself, she sank to the floor and began to cry, letting the sobs that shook her body overcome her.

She loved Sal so much, and all this time he'd been lying to her. In his own way, Sal had betrayed her the same way her husband had. She'd told Sal that when she married again—*if* she married again—she wanted the kind of marriage she hadn't had with Tony. She wanted a different kind of man and a different kind of marriage. What she'd wanted was Sal. But that was before she knew how easy it was for him to deceive her.

For one brief, shining moment she'd thought Sal was the man to share those dreams with, to share her life with; but that moment was shattered when she learned of his deception. No wonder Sal thought she needed someone to look after her; she couldn't even tell when a man was lying to her. If Sal had kept something like this from her in order to protect Tony, what else had he kept from her?

An overwhelming sense of sadness etched itself into her heart as she realized once again what a fool she'd been. She'd trusted her husband, and he had betrayed her. It hurt, but Tony was gone now. What he did explained a lot of things—things she'd never understood. She felt a wave of sadness for the man who'd once been her husband. They probably shouldn't even have married in the first place. They'd never had a deep burning love. It was more like two lonely people drifting toward one another for comfort.

Her love for Sal was different; it was fire and heat and an intense longing to always be with him. She'd waited her whole life to feel this way about a man. It had been a long, often lonely wait. And for what?

Tears filled her eyes again and a quiet desperation filled her soul. She was quite certain she'd never felt so alone in her life. Alone and lonely. She loved Sal as she'd never loved anyone else, but how could she ever trust him again?

Annie smiled sadly. The answer was simple. She couldn't.

Chapter Ten

It had been a week, and Sal was growing impatient. He knew he had to give Annie time, but his heart ached for what she was going through—for what *he*'d put her through. He knew she was going to be hurt, he'd expected it. What he hadn't expected was the absolute devastation he felt.

She refused his calls, and every time he stopped at the deli she scurried out the back door, avoiding him. He was going nuts. The past week had been torture. Never had he known such agony, such bleakness. In seven long, lonely days he'd learned he needed Annie just as he needed air to breathe.

Stabbing anxiety dogged his steps. He was cross and short-tempered at work, barking orders and being a general pain in the behind. This morning the captain had threatened him with suspension if he didn't get his act together. Sal knew he had to do something.

Somehow, he had to find a way to make her understand.

He had a plan but he'd need some help. During lunch he called his mother and his aunt. They agreed to pass the word and do whatever they could. By late that afternoon, his plan was in motion. The rest was up to Annie.

"Annie," Rosina said gently. "Salvatore called. Again."

"And what did you tell him?" she finally asked, because Rosina was just standing there looking at her with such a hopeful expression. If she didn't answer her, Rosina wouldn't get back to work, and then they would have twenty-five people standing at the counter listening to the life and times of poor Annie Milano, the notorious widow woman.

"The same thing I've been telling him for a week." Rosina patted her shoulder, her dark eyes somber. "I've never seen my Salvatore like this. I'm so worried. He loves you, Annie," Rosina said. "And you love him. I don't know why you two don't stop this foolishness."

Foolishness. Annie smiled sadly. She knew just who the fool had been. A week ago the thought that Sal loved her would have filled her with ecstasy. Now it just filled her with an aching sadness. For a week, Rosina, Florina and even Mrs. Altero had been pleading Sal's case, insisting he'd only been trying to protect her because he loved her. Annie was trying hard not to let them wear down her resistance; she was trying not to let herself believe Sal really cared. If he did, how could he have lied to her for two years?

Banishing such thoughts, Annie turned to her waiting customer, mentally noting his sandwich preference, then quickly went about filling his order. She'd never been so grateful for the deli or its distractions. She'd thrown herself into her work, dragging herself home every night, falling into bed exhausted, but unable to sleep.

One week. She hadn't seen or talked to Sal in seven long days. It was the longest period of time in two years she had gone without seeing him. His absence left a crater-size hole in her life.

She'd done nothing but think and cry, and then get mad. But the past was done and over. She couldn't do anything about it now. But it didn't make it hurt any less, or make her feel any less a fool.

Now she had to face the future, knowing she would face it alone. She'd learned to go on once before, and she could do it again. But, oh, how she missed Sal. He was a part of her, a part she couldn't seem to let go of. Not seeing him didn't ease the loneliness. He was in her mind and in her heart, and always would be.

She had to come to terms with the fact that her whole life had been a lie. She no longer knew whom or what to believe. Shame burned her cheeks.

The man she thought loved her, didn't. The man she thought she could trust, she couldn't. Perhaps that was what hurt the most: the fact that Sal had betrayed her. She'd let herself fall in love with him and then found out that in his own way, he'd lied and deceived her. So much for her own good judgment about men.

Sal's absence was obvious. Not everyone had known what had happened, but still they all rallied around her, giving her love and support just as they always had. Mr. Finucci had even invited her to the movies again, this time offering to pay. And Mr. Benedetto stopped by every evening during his walk to invite her along. Rosina and Florina hovered around her, watching and waiting. She loved them all, but this was something she had to handle on her own.

She moved to the register, offering her customer a smile and making change for his twenty. Mrs. Altero came into the store, smiling and waving.

"Annie, I've just made some wonderful prune pudding. Why don't you come over and try some?"

Annie's stomach rippled. Mrs. Altero had been trying to tempt her—or poison her—with gastronomical oddities all week. Annie steadfastly refused. Of all the things that would make her feel better, prune pudding was definitely not high on the list. "I'd love to," Annie lied, softening her words with a smile. "But I can't." She nodded toward the line at the register. "I've got my hands full here and will probably have to work late."

"Sal's coming for dinner, tonight." Mrs. Altero sighed happily. "My granddaughter's been dying to—" Mrs. Altero slapped a hand over her mouth as Annie's head snapped up. Her eyes glistened for a moment.

"I'm sorry," Mrs. Altero whispered, shaking her head. "I forgot. I didn't mean—"

Annie came around the counter to comfort the woman. "It's all right, Mrs. Altero. Sal's got a right to live his own life," she lied, suddenly brimming with jealousy.

Smooth, Suave Sal. Her temper simmered. It sure hadn't taken him any time to get back into the groove. Obviously, what had happened between them meant very little to him. He was just carrying on with his life as if nothing had happened. Well, so could she!

"I hope he gets indigestion," Annie muttered testily, going back around the counter to finish helping her waiting customers.

Once everyone had been taken care of and the deli was quiet again, Annie glanced around. She felt an overwhelming sadness, mixed with love. Everything was so familiar, so much the same, but so changed. Her life was so empty without Sal.

Despite what Sal had done, she knew she would never stop loving him. Her heart flipped over just thinking of him. With Sal, what she felt was fire and heat and an intense longing to be with him forever.

The knowledge of her love for him only added to her despair. Annie suddenly felt bone tired, wishing the day would end.

She worked quietly, dusting shelves, placing orders for stock, doing her books. Late in the day she glanced up from the register to see a dark blue sedan pull up to the curb across the street. Her heart began to pound. She only knew one person who drove that kind of car. Fumbling with the cash drawer, she slammed it shut, waiting to see if he would come in.

Holding her breath, she pretended to be deeply engrossed in a case of tomatoes that had just arrived, looking up every time the door opened, hoping against hope it would be him. But after several long minutes, Annie realized he wasn't going to come in, he wasn't even going to try to see her. He was going to have dinner with Mrs. Altero's granddaughter.

"Annie, Florina and I have some things to do this afternoon. Would you mind if we left?"

Annie glanced up at Rosina in surprise. In all the years the twins had worked for her, they'd never asked to leave early. It was odd.

"No, of course not." She watched the twins whispering as they pulled off their aprons and collected their handbags.

Annie worked quietly, occasionally glancing up. Near dusk, she looked up to find Mr. Benedetto carrying a large case of fruit into Mrs. Altero's house. Annie frowned. What on earth was going on? Sal's car was still parked outside, along with half a dozen others. Annie felt a twinge of hurt. Something was going on in the neighborhood, something that she obviously hadn't been included in.

After checking all the doors and filling out her bank receipts, Annie let herself out the back door and headed for home. The house seemed oddly empty, and after brewing a pot of tea she took it into the living room, pulling up the rocker to stare out the window.

She wasn't watching for Sal, she assured herself, frowning at the flurry of activity going on across the street. Florina and Rosina went hustling in the door, followed by Mr. Finucci. Annie frowned. What the devil was going on?

Sipping her tea, she couldn't help but wonder what Sal was doing.

Oh, Sal, she thought sadly. Why couldn't you have been honest with me? Why couldn't you just have told me about Tony? She'd thought a lot about Tony the past week. In some ways she understood why he'd done what he'd done. Their relationship would never be classified as a great love. It was quiet, comfortable. He'd been clearly as unhappy as she had been. Maybe *unhappy* wasn't the right word. Perhaps it was *uneasy*. She'd cared for Tony deeply, but she'd loved him more as a friend than a lover. What he'd done hurt, but she understood. He was the one who'd ultimately suffered the most; he'd lost his life as a result of his foolishness. Poor Tony.

She'd spent hours and hours this past week sitting by the open window and wondering why Sal hadn't told her the truth. He'd said he'd done it to protect her, because he hadn't wanted to hurt her any further.

Could that really be the reason? she wondered. Or had he simply been protecting Tony? Annie wasn't sure anymore, and her head hurt from trying to figure it out. Whatever his reasons, all she knew was that she still loved him, and always would.

"Hey, Annie," Sal called. "You waiting for someone?"

Startled, she jumped from the chair. Sal was standing beneath the open window, grinning up at her. She wondered how long he'd been standing there, watching her. She also wondered how he could look so good when she felt so miserable. Worn jeans clung to his powerful legs. A white sweatshirt spread wide across his muscular shoulders. His face had healed—most of the bruises were just faint shadows—but his eyes looked lonely.

Her breath scampered at the sight of him as her eyes feasted on him. It had been so long since she'd seen him, touched him, kissed him. Her heart ached with loneliness for him.

Oh, Sal.

"No, I am not," she lied stiffly, trying to calm the pounding of her heart. "What's going on at Mrs. Altero's?" she asked suddenly, and Sal grinned.

"Come on down and I'll tell you."

"I can hear you from here, Sal."

"Are you still angry at me?" he called, climbing up the stairs.

"I was never angry," she said slowly. "I think hurt would be more accurate." Annie shrugged. "What's done is done, Sal. I'm sure you had your reasons for what you did at the time. There's nothing we can do to change things now." She glanced at his profile, loving him, loving everything about him. She'd thought what she wanted was to be independent, not to lean on him anymore. But now, faced with the reality of what she'd wished for, Annie realized it wasn't what she wanted, after all. What she wanted was Sal. But it was too late; she knew that now.

"Annie," he began quietly, needing to clear the air between them once and for all. "I know now what I did was wrong. I should have told you the truth about everything right from the beginning. But I didn't. What I did, I did to protect you, not hurt you. You've got to know, Annie, I'd never do anything in this world to hurt you."

She nodded as her eyes filled with tears. No, Sal never would do anything to hurt anyone—not deliberately, anyway. In his own old-fashioned way, he thought what he was doing was right. His intentions were honorable, it was just his actions that were out of kilter. How could she hold it against him for trying to protect her? Annie realized now that she couldn't.

"I know you'd never hurt me deliberately," she said quietly, wishing things were different. She had some pride left. Her love for him and her memories were something she would always have—that was more than some people ever had. Oh, Lord. All this time she'd thought she wanted to be independent. But now she realized, when it was too late, that the harder she fought for her independence, the more she really needed him and loved him.

"So what's going on across the street? What's all the commotion?"

"They're...uh...planning a wedding," he said with a grin.

"A wedding!" Annie looked at him carefully. "Who's getting married?"

"I am."

Her eyes flew to his and she almost dropped her teacup out the window. "You're *what*?" she croaked, feeling her heart constrict with pain. Her eyes slid closed. So Mrs. Altero's granddaughter had finally captured Smooth, Suave Sal. Oh, Lord. What was she going to do?

"Getting married," he said slowly, drawing out the words. "You know—love, honor and obey, and all that other good stuff."

Annie looked at him skeptically. She just couldn't imagine him getting married. "When is this...wedding supposed to take place?"

Sal grinned. "I was thinking about tomorrow night. Ryce knows a judge who can perform a private service. I've invited everyone from the neighborhood."

"Everyone in the neighborhood!" she cried. "I'm so glad I'm the last one to know, as usual," she snapped.

"Well, to tell you the truth, Annie, I wasn't quite sure how you'd react—do you like children?" he asked abruptly and Annie turned to him, her eyes blazing.

"Now what do my feelings for children have to do with you getting married?"

"Well, we've talked about everything else the past two years, but we've never discussed how you felt about kids. See, I'd like to have about six, but I can't do it by myself. I'll need some help, so I thought it was a good idea to find out how you felt about kids before we get married. Of course, if you don't like kids, we—"

"Before...we...*what*?" She looked at him incredulously, waiting for his words to sink in.

"Before we get married," he called out. "You're always saying I should tell you things, so I figured, I'd better tell you *before* the wedding that I'd like to have kids rather than after. It seems much simpler, don't you think?"

"Don't *I* think," she cried. "Are you crazy, Sal? You think you can just show up here—after you've been on a date with another woman, I might add— and—"

"I love you, Annie," he called to her, a wide smile on his face. "I want you to marry me—tomorrow night, if you're not busy."

"If I'm not busy?" Annie stared at him for long silent moments, letting his words sink in. Oh, Lord! He loved her and wanted her to marry him—tomorrow night. This time Annie did drop her teacup, and fled out the door. She ran full tilt into his arms. Sal cocked his head and looked at her, his lips curving in a smile. Their eyes met. Annie stared up at him, her heart filled with love and joy as a full smile lifted her lips.

"Uh, Annie, yoo-hoo!" He waved a hand in her face until she blinked back to reality. "I know I don't have much experience with this love stuff, but I think when a man tells you he loves you, it's customary to say something in return."

"You love me?" she repeated incredulously, and Sal shook his head.

"That's not what you're supposed to say," he scolded, lifting her arms and settling them around his neck. "Now, Annie, repeat after me, I love you, Sal— You do love me, don't you?" he asked worriedly, and Annie laughed softly, tightening her arms around him.

"Yes, I love you," she confirmed, watching his grin slide wider.

"And you're going to marry me, right?"

"But what about Mrs. Altero's granddaughter? I thought—I just assumed—" His lips covered hers, stopping her words. With a sigh of pleasure, Annie slipped her arms around him, leaning against him and welcoming his touch. Sal loved her!

Angling his head, he settled his lips firmly over hers. Her senses reeled in delight and her own hands moved restlessly, gently roaming his broad back and shoulders.

Annie clung to him, whimpering softly at the yearning he awakened in her. His lips moved relentlessly over hers, possessive and demanding. His soft tongue gently teased her, demanding she respond in kind. Her breathing came fast and heavily, causing her breasts to rise and fall against his chest.

Sal slowly traced the length of her spine with his fingertips. "Annie," Sal breathed, pulling his mouth free. There was a huskiness in his voice she hadn't heard before. The rapid rate of his breathing matched her own.

Sal draped his arm around her shoulder and pulled her close, nuzzling her hair. "Oh, Annie, how could you ever think I'd let you go? I've waited my whole life for you." He drew back and looked at her, letting his hands caress her.

She met his gaze, her eyes shining with love. There was a loud round of applause, and Annie and Sal turned to find most of the neighborhood hanging out Mrs. Altero's window, watching them.

Annie and Sal chuckled softly. "We're going to have a big old-fashioned Italian wedding," he informed her, tightening his arms around her. "I've invited everybody—"

"Except the bride," she reminded him, trying not to grin.

"Except the bride," he confirmed.

"We're not really getting married tomorrow, are we?"

Sal grinned and nodded his head. "I love you, Annie. I don't think I can wait any longer. I've waited far too long for you as it is."

"But Sal," she protested. "I haven't done anything. I need a dress and shoes, and there's food to prepare. How can I possibly get everything done in less than twenty-four hours?"

"You don't have to do a thing but show up," he announced, grinning at the perplexed look on her face. "Everything's been taken care of. That's what all the commotion has been about. My mother and aunt have been working all afternoon. We'll get married around six; I thought we could do it in your living room if you don't mind—" He waited for her nod of approval. "I've already got permission to close off the street for the evening." He grinned. "See, I told you everything was taken care of."

"But what about attendants, and a dress, and a ring, and—" Sal pressed his fingers to her lips to silence her.

"What do you think I've been doing the past week? Ryce is going to be my best man. As for attendants, would you mind if my mother and aunt stood up for you?"

"I'd love it," Annie said with a laugh, wondering why she hadn't thought of it sooner.

"Mr. Finucci promised to keep his hands to himself if you let him give you away, and as for a ring..." Smiling, Sal dug into the pocket of his jeans. "Now, Ann Marie Milano," he said, going down on one knee, "we're going to do this right." He took her hand in his, looking up at her with such love, her heart almost burst with happiness. "Will you marry me?"

Tears blurred her vision and she nodded her head. "Yes, Salvatore, I'll marry you."

Sal turned and flashed a thumbs-up signal to the assembled group, and a loud burst of applause and cheering filled the night air, causing Annie to blush. It seemed fitting. Everyone in the neighborhood was like family. They'd shared so much of her sadness, it was only right they shared her joy.

Sal took her hand and slipped a small ruby ring on her finger. Annie gasped softly.

"Sal, that's your mother's ring." She examined the delicate gold design carefully. Rosina had worn the ring for as long as Annie could remember.

"No, Annie, it's *your* ring. That ring belonged to my great-grandfather and has been passed down for three generations. My father gave it to my mother when they got engaged, and when we have a son, we'll pass it to him to give to his bride-to-be."

"Oh, Sal," she breathed quietly, touched beyond measure. "It's beautiful." He leaned forward and brushed his lips across hers.

"Salvatore," Rosina called, shaking her finger at him. "It's bad luck to see the bride the night before the wedding."

Sal pulled his lips free. "Annie," he groaned softly. "You wouldn't believe what I've been through this past week. I don't ever want to go another day without seeing you, or touching you. I love you, Annie. I love you and I want to spend the rest of my life with you. I promise never to withhold anything from you again. You have to trust me, Annie, do you think you can do that?" Sal held his breath and waited.

"Yes, Sal," she said quietly, sliding her arms around his waist and laying her head on his shoulder. "I do trust you. I think I understand why you did what you did, but Sal, I couldn't take it if you ever..." She couldn't put into words her fears, but she sensed that Sal understood.

"Lied to you?" he finished for her and she expelled a sigh of relief. "Annie, that's something you don't ever have to worry about ever again. I know now I should have just told you the truth. I want the kind of marriage we talked about, the kind where we share everything—the good and the bad." He bent and brushed his lips across hers again.

"It's bad luck, Salvatore!" Rosina called again, and Sal and Annie grinned.

"Annie," he murmured, looking down at her. "You never told me how you felt about kids?"

"I love them," she admitted. "The more the merrier."

"Good. That's going to be the first thing on the agenda—after the wedding," he clarified when he saw the look on her face. "I have to think of my honor," he teased, capturing her face in his hands. "I love you, Ann Marie Milano soon-to-be Giordiano," he whispered, and she smiled.

"And I love you, too, Sal."

He bent and kissed her forehead. "Until tomorrow?"

She nodded, settling for one brief kiss before letting him go. "Until tomorrow."

By five o'clock the next evening Annie's house was packed with guests. She paced the length of her bedroom, nervous as a cat. Her wedding dress was the simple white silk dress she'd worn the night they had gone to Parillo's. The pearl-handled combs served as her headpiece and Mrs. Altero had picked a bouquet of summer flowers for her to carry. Everything was done, and now they were just waiting for the groom.

Florina swept into the room, followed closely by Rosina who kept dabbing at her eyes. "Oh, Annie," Rosina said wistfully, "you look so beautiful." The twins were dressed identically in the palest shade of blue. It was the first time Annie had ever seen them in anything other than their somber black dresses.

"Thank you," Annie murmured, listening to the commotion from downstairs. "You two look beautiful, too." Annie frowned. "What's going on down there?" she inquired, growing more worried by the second.

"Humph!" Florina huffed. "Mrs. Altero made these little sandwiches for the guests to munch on while they wait. Last time I looked, everyone was scurrying around trying to find a place to dump them. After the wedding, we're going to have to search the house for those little lead balls!" Annie couldn't help but laugh at the expression on the older woman's face.

"Is Sal here, yet?" she asked, and Rosina smiled.

"He's here, sent us up to see if you're all right."

"No, he didn't, sister," Florina corrected. "He sent us up to make sure she hadn't changed her mind. You haven't, have you?" Florina inquired, leaning close.

"I haven't changed my mind—" Annie laughed "—and I'm fine. Just a bit anxious to get going."

There was a sharp rap at the door and Rosina went to answer it. Mr. Finucci stood in the doorway, dressed in splendor. His dark suit was new, his hair was freshly cut, and his shoes were polished to a high sheen. Even his cane was new. It was long and black, with a pearl handle.

"It's time," he grumbled, looking at Annie and extending his arm. Taking a deep breath, Annie had one last look in the mirror and reached for Mr. Finucci's arm.

Yes, Annie realized, it was time.

"Let's go," she said softly as the opening strains of the wedding march filtered up the stairs. Rosina and Florina began their descent, followed by Annie and Mr. Finucci. Annie held her breath as she walked, smiling as Mr. Finucci patted her hand in encouragement.

Her breath caught when she saw Sal, dressed in a dark gray suit, crisp white shirt and red silk tie. She was certain he'd never looked more handsome. Their eyes met and held, and Annie smiled.

Mr. Finucci kissed her gently on the cheek, then presented her to Sal. Tears filled Annie's eyes at the look on Sal's face. "Are you ready, hon?" he asked softly, taking her hand and giving it a squeeze.

Annie nodded. "I'm ready."

"I love you," Sal whispered, leaning forward to kiss her. Annie forgot about the guests and the judge and everyone else but the man in her arms. She held him tight, giving him all she had to give.

Ryce cleared his throat. "Umm...Sal?" After a few moments, Ryce tapped Sal on the shoulder. "Sal!" he hissed. "I believe it's customary to wait until *after* the ceremony to kiss the bride."

Pulling away, Sal grinned as the guests broke into laughter. Tucking Annie's hand in his arm, he turned to the judge. "We're ready," Sal said, and Annie smiled, her heart filled with love. Yes, they were ready. Rosina was right; it was time. For both of them.

Epilogue

Annie?" Sal whispered, brushing a tumble of dark curls off her face. "Are you still sleeping?" He nuzzled her lips gently with his. She sighed softly and wrapped her arms around her husband.

"Not anymore," she murmured with a contented smile. Her lashes fluttered closed again as Sal's mouth found hers. All too soon, Sal pulled his lips from hers, causing her to groan in protest.

"Where are you going?" she asked as Sal slid out of bed.

"I've got a date," he whispered, leaning over to kiss her gently on the forehead. Her eyes sprung open and she bolted upright, taking the sheet with her.

"You've got a what!" she cried in alarm.

"A date, honey," he repeated, his eyes twinkling with mischief. "I sure wouldn't want to disappoint Gina."

"Gina!" Annie scrambled out of bed, dragging the sheet along with her. "Who the hell is Gina?" she demanded, following him around the room as he gathered his clothes.

"Don't swear, Ann Marie," Sal scolded, trying not to smile at the harassed look on her face.

"Don't swear!" she cried. "You announce you've got a date twenty-four hours after we get married, and you're telling me not to swear! Sal—wait—where are you going?" She stomped after him. "Who is Gina?"

"Gina," he said sweetly, "is Mrs. Altero's granddaughter." He grinned at her. "You're not upset, are you?"

"I'll give you upset!" she cried, hauling off to whack him on the arm. "Didn't anyone ever tell you that dating is not part of the marriage contract!"

"It's not?" he said, doing his best to look perplexed. The doorbell rang, and Sal hurriedly stepped into his jeans. "There she is." He leaned down to peck Annie on the cheek. "Love you, but I'd better hurry. I wouldn't want to keep Gina waiting."

"Keep *her* waiting!" Clutching the sheet around her, Annie stomped after him, wishing she had Florina's bat right now. "Wait until I get my hands on you, Sal Giordiano," she muttered, trying to hang on to the sheet and get down the stairs at the same time.

At the bottom of the steps Annie came to an abrupt halt. Her eyes widened in surprise and she clutched the sheet tighter around her. Sal was down on one knee talking to a little girl of about twelve with the most enormous brown eyes she'd ever seen.

Sal turned to look at her, his eyes twinkling with amusement. "Annie, I'd like you to meet Gina." He stood up and took the child by the hand. "This is Mrs. Altero's granddaughter."

Annie blinked, looking from one to other. "This is Mrs. Altero's granddaughter?" she repeated numbly, and the child smiled and stepped forward.

"Hello, Mrs. Giordiano. It's a pleasure to meet you."

Annie took the child's hand and shook it solemnly. She glanced up at Sal who stood grinning from ear to ear.

"Gina couldn't come to the wedding because she had a stomachache, so I promised her we'd take her to the zoo today."

"My grandma made stuffed cabbage," Gina said, wrinkling her nose. "And I always get a stomachache from it. I still don't feel very well, so could we go to the zoo another day?" She turned to Sal.

"Sure, honey, anytime you want."

"Grandma wants to know if you'd like to come for dinner tonight?"

"No!" Annie and Sal caroled in alarm. "We've made plans already," Sal lied, opening the door for the little girl. "But thank your grandmother for us, anyway." Sal closed the door behind Gina and heaved a sigh of relief, until his eyes landed on Annie. He grinned.

"Uh-oh," he murmured, as she advanced on him, clutching the sheet tightly around her. "Now, Annie," he said, holding his hands in the air and backing away from her.

"You think you're pretty funny, don't you," she accused, smiling broadly. "All this time you let me believe—"

"Now, Annie," Sal said with a laugh, grabbing her around the waist and scooping her up in his arms. "*I* didn't do anything. *I* never said Gina was— It's your own fault— You're not mad, are you?" He looked down at her, his eyes filled with love. "I love you, Annie," he whispered, bending to brush his lips across hers. She wrapped her arms around his neck.

"I love you, too," she whispered, her breath shuddering through her lips. "But no more *dates*!"

He grinned. "Honey, the only date I'm interested in is a due date. Think we can work on a baby?" he inquired hopefully, and Annie laughed.

"I thought that's what we were doing last night," she teased, nibbling at his ear. Sal groaned softly and headed up the stairs.

"It was," he assured her. "But you know what they say—practice makes perfect!"

* * * * *

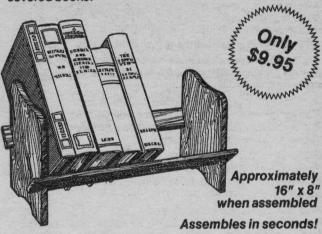

COMING NEXT MONTH

#616 TO MARRY AT CHRISTMAS—Kasey Michaels
Elizabeth Chatham wasn't looking for romance . . . until she met dynamic Nicholas Lancaster and fell head over heels. Would wedding bells harmonize with sleigh bells?

#617 AFTER THE STORM—Joan Smith
Aspiring writer Susan Knight was more than curious about her mysterious new neighbor, Dan Ogilvy. She had to discover what the sexiest man she'd ever met was up to. . . .

#618 IF DREAMS WERE WILD HORSES—Adeline McElfresh
Ana-Maureen Salem thought she was fenced into her city life. But then she bought a wild horse and met Jeremy Rodriguez—the one man who could let her passion run free!

#619 THE KERANDRAON LEGACY—Sara Grant
The legacy of a magnificent Breton mansion stood between them, but one magical moonlit night Christie Beaumont lost her heart forever to devastating Luc Keraven. . . .

#620 A MAN OF HER OWN—Brenda Trent
Widow Kaye Wilson dreamed of building a life for herself and her daughter—without the help of a man. Then she met irresistible Whit Brooks. . . .

#621 CACTUS ROSE—Stella Bagwell
Years after he'd left her, rugged Tony Ramirez returned to help lovely Andrea Rawlins save her ranch. Could Andrea risk loving this masterful Texan again?

AVAILABLE THIS MONTH:

#610 ITALIAN KNIGHTS
Sharon De Vita

#611 A WOMAN OF SPIRIT
Lucy Gordon

#612 NOVEMBER RETURNS
Octavia Street

#613 FIVE-ALARM AFFAIR
Marie Ferrarella

#614 THE DISCERNING HEART
Arlene James

#615 GUARDIAN ANGEL
Nicole Monet

FOUR UNIQUE SERIES FOR EVERY WOMAN YOU ARE...

Silhouette Romance

Love, at its most tender, provocative, emotional ... in stories that will make you laugh and cry while bringing you the magic of falling in love.

6 titles per month

Silhouette Special Edition

Sophisticated, substantial and packed with emotion, these powerful novels of life and love will capture your imagination and steal your heart.

6 titles per month

Silhouette Desire

Open the door to romance and passion. Humorous, emotional, compelling—yet always a believable and sensuous story—Silhouette Desire never fails to deliver on the promise of love.

6 titles per month

Silhouette Intimate Moments

Enter a world of excitement, of romance heightened by suspense, adventure and the passions every woman dreams of. Let us sweep you away.

4 titles per month

SILG-1R